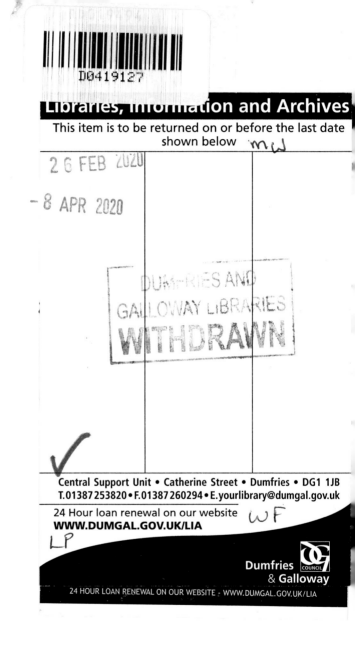

MONTANA MANHUNT

Rush Bonner's horse is stolen in mighty wild country. But Bonner is tough: he recovers his mount and leaves the thieving rider for the coyotes. But this brings him more trouble. First, there is the head wound and the jail cell. Then the escape — with a dead sheriff left in his office, and ten thousand dollars missing. The posse hunting him has orders to 'Take him, dead or alive — preferably dead.' He surely wishes he'd stayed in Texas!

HANK J. KIRBY

MONTANA MANHUNT

Complete and Unabridged

LINFORD
Leicester

First published in Great Britain in 2008 by
Robert Hale Limited
London

First Linford Edition
published 2009
by arrangement with
Robert Hale Limited
London

The moral right of the author has been asserted

British Library CIP Data

Kirby, Hank J.
    Montana manhunt - -
    (Linford western library)
    1. Western stories.
    2. Large type books.
    I. Title II. Series
    823.9′2–dc22

ISBN 978–1–84782–736–4

Published by
F. A. Thorpe (Publishing)
Anstey, Leicestershire

Set by Words & Graphics Ltd.
Anstey, Leicestershire
Printed and bound in Great Britain by
T. J. International Ltd., Padstow, Cornwall

This book is printed on acid-free paper

1

'Who is he?'

Something broke the line of the razorback hill where it seemed to lean against the lowering sky. A small ripple of movement, briefly blurring the definition of the crest.

Marty Rice saw it and reined down her buckskin, swinging slightly left. She threw a quick glance at the ambling herd, checking that her three riders were in position. Then she tilted her hat forward slightly so that the broad brim shaded her blue eyes and gave the razorback her closer attention.

There it was again, this side now, just below the crest, and clear enough for her to make out a horseman. A *hurt* horseman, judging by the way he was slumped forward over the neck of what looked like a roan mount.

1

Her face was caked with dust and she wiped the back of a gloved hand across her lips, moistened them slightly with her tongue, then whistled sharply through her teeth.

Flapjack, riding drag, was closest and heard her. He turned lazily and she made gestures towards the hill. By then he had seen the swaying rider making a precarious descent. He stood in the stirrups, shading his eyes with one hand.

'Want me to go check him out?' Ready and willing.

She shook her head, emphasizing the negative with a sweep of her left hand. 'He's hurt — in no condition to give trouble.'

'Might be touchy or out of his head — I better go.'

'Stay!'

He knew that crackling sharpness in her voice and eased back in his saddle, waving acknowledgement, but, at the same time, easing his rifle in the scabbard.

2

She had already wheeled the buck-skin, touched the spurs to the sweaty, dusty hide and lifted the mount to a gallop. She angled towards the foot of the razorback, shoulder-length dark hair flying, judging where the rider would leave the slope.

Flapjack, young and still full of chivalry, stood in the stirrups again, frowning, heart beating just a little faster. He saw her intercept the rider, lean down and grab the roan's bridle. The horse skidded and swayed and the wounded man toppled from the saddle.

Flapjack was already lifting his own mount to a run when she dismounted, knelt, then stood and waved her hat urgently for him to join her.

Feller must be pretty badly hurt, he decided as he rode in, easing the rifle clear of the scabbard now. He levered a load into the breech as his grey eyes swept the razorback's slopes.

A wounded man might still have someone on his backtrail.

He quit saddle while his horse was

still skidding, bringing his rifle across his chest, even as he saw the man in dusty, worn clothes lying at Marty's feet. He looked long and lean, face streaked with rivulets of blood.

'He's been headshot.' Marty wrenched off her neckerchief and began wiping away some of the blood. 'We'll have to get him to a doctor.'

Flapjack nodded absently, looking up towards the crest, tightening his grip on the Winchester.

'Hope whoever shot him ain't still up there.'

* * *

The doctor stepped back from the narrow infirmary bed and looked down at his new patient, now with his head swathed in a clean white bandage. He turned slightly to look at Marty Rice, gestured to a battered, dirt-caked hat and what looked like part of a bloody shirt on a table.

'He had enough sense to jam that

cloth over the wound with his hat to slow the bleeding. Which means he wasn't knocked out right away by the bullet.'

'You sound a bit surprised, Doctor.'

He nodded, a middle-sized man, shirt buttoned to a flabby neck, no collar, his face round and red. 'Gouge is pretty deep. Showing a patch of bone in one area.'

Marty frowned. She was in her mid-twenties, not very tall, but even her trail-stained workclothes of faded shirt and frayed denim trousers tucked into scuffed half boots, showed she had a good form. Her face, patchy because of the trail dust and sunburn, still was pleasant, her eyes clear like the blue Montana sky showing through the window. Her hat had plastered her brown hair to her head a little, but the natural waves were beginning already to lift it slightly.

'He moaned once or twice on the way in but didn't regain full consciousness.'

'No — who is he?'

'No idea. I sent one of my men to the sheriff with the bedroll and saddle-bags that were on the roan — there should be some identification amongst his things.'

'His hands are calloused, showing a couple of rope burns — I'd say he's a cowboy, probably on the drift.'

'He has at least one enemy,' she said quietly.

'So it would seem.'

'Will he recover?'

'I should think so. He's well muscled, though lean. And that square jaw speaks of inner strength as well.'

'But . . . ?'

He looked at her sharply and his thick lips moved slightly in a smile. 'But — I don't like that wound. Of course, everyone has a different thickness of the skull bone, but there's been a sliver shaved off. It could have depressed the bone on to the brain which may affect — well, many things.'

She grimaced briefly, glancing again

6

at the wounded stranger. 'It sounds serious. I hope he pulls through, Doctor. I'll have to go see about my herd, but I'll try and look in again before I leave town.'

As she turned towards the door, it opened and a large man, breathing wheezily, came in quickly. A sheriff's star glinted briefly on his worn and faded vest.

Kit Pollard was a middle-aged man, obviously had some kind of breathing problem. He nodded curtly to the girl and the doctor. His eyes slid quickly to the stranger with the bandaged head. 'He come to yet, Doc?'

'Not yet, Kit, and I don't think I can make a guess about when he might come round. It could be in one minute, an hour or a day. Perhaps even longer.'

'Or not at all?'

'We-ell, the behaviour of head wounds is hard to predict.'

The lawman's lips tightened. He glanced again at Marty who was making no move to leave now, sensing something in the sheriff's attitude. It made her curious.

'Did you find anything in his gear, Sheriff?'

He smiled thinly. 'Found somethin'. Nothin' to say who he is, but he ain't short of money.' He waited, letting that sink in, before adding, 'Bottoms of both saddle-bags are lined with bills — totalling almost ten thousand dollars.'

That startled both the doctor and Marty Rice.

'That's a . . . slew of money, Kit!'

'That it is, Doc, and there's some gold double eagles in a small canvas drawstring poke as well — labelled as belongin' to the State Bank at Miller's Ford.'

Marty gasped, and her hand went to her mouth. 'Isn't that the bank that was robbed a couple of weeks ago?'

Sheriff Pollard nodded, face grim now as he looked at the man in the bed. 'Yeah. Big shoot-out, two lawmen and a townsman killed, woman and child hurt in the getaway, run down, some say deliberately. And the gang got away, all of 'em.'

'Not all — I killed one after he . . . bushwhacked me and stole my horse.'

All attention snapped to the wounded man, whose eyes were open now, as he lay there, staring at them, chest heaving with the effort of talking.

As the doctor hurried to the bedside, Kit Pollard, face tight, said, 'Now, mebbe you better tell me about that, mister.'

2

A Man Called Rush

He said his name was Rush Bonner.

Just at that time, Pollard's deputy, Dean Halstead came into the room. He topped six feet easy and weighed around 180 pounds — 179 of it pure hard muscle. The deputy had a tough, thin-lipped face, not unattractive, and pale-grey eyes that fixed to the stranger's face now.

'Rush? Where the hell'd you get a name like that?'

'Same place you got yours, I guess,' Bonner replied, straining a little. 'Parents picked it.'

Dean Halstead curled a thin lip. 'My mother named me after her father: General Clinton Dean. You must've heard of him.'

'Believe that Yankee got a brief

mention in the Cavalry *Handbook*.'

Halstead scowled, glanced at the sheriff. 'I thought I heard a Reb accent there. Where you from, Bonner? Good ol' Takes-us?'

'Brazos country.'

He tried to struggle to a sitting position and the doctor moved to help, Marty going to the other side and taking his arm, lifting. In a few struggling moments they had Rush Bonner half upright with several pillows behind him. Panting, the man looked at Halstead.

'My pappy always said I came into this life in a rush; fifteen minutes labour and there I was.'

Halstead grunted and started to speak but the medico interrupted. 'Kit, d'you have to question him now? Mr Bonner should rest. Not necessarily sleep, but rest. Quiet.'

'Doc, I need to know where all that money in his saddle-bags came from. Sooner the better.'

Bonner looked a trifle surprised at

the mention of money, but slightly lifted one hand. 'Gimme a shot of whiskey, Doc. I'll be OK.'

The doctor hesitated, but brought a bottle of whiskey in from another room and poured some into a glass. Bonner glanced at him, still holding the glass out, and the doctor sighed as he added more.

'This your preferred medicine, Mr Bonner?'

Bonner drank half of it, coughed a little and blew out his cheeks as he shook his head. 'Only at times like this. Doc, you got something for a headache?'

The sheriff and deputy were obviously impatient as a pain-killing draught was prepared and Bonner drank it down.

'You start to feel dizzy . . . ' began the doctor and Bonner again held up his hand.

'I'll know when to stop.' He settled his gaze on Marty. 'I got to thank you, ma'am. I came round briefly in that *travois* you had your men make for me, but just couldn't bring myself to talk right then.'

'How about now?' snapped the sheriff testily. Bonner nodded slowly.

'This first: they ain't my saddle-bags. We can go into it later, if you like, but right now, here's what happened: I left Bozeman on the fourteenth — '

'That would be almost a week ago,' the girl said.

Bonner flicked his eyes to her but continued, 'and headed east, aiming to cross the Yellowstone between Livingstone and Big Timber. But there'd been a lot of rain and the river was flooding, so I headed north, still this side of the river, which took a wide swing around. I figured that was the best way out: extra miles but no need to cross.'

'Didn't try at Miller's Ford?' Kit Pollard asked casually, but his eyes alert.

Bonner smiled faintly. 'Never went anywheres near Miller's Ford. 'Fact I've never been there at all.'

'Sure,' broke in Halstead. 'You just found that money a'floatin' downstream and put it in your saddle-bags to keep it safe.'

Despite the pain he must be suffering, Bonner's eyes seemed to drop a sort of blind and the blue changed to something cold and flat. Halstead saw it and frowned.

'You keep interrupting, this is gonna take all day.'

'The hell it will,' the sheriff growled, snapping a hard look at the big deputy. 'Just hush up, Dean.'

Marty and the others saw that Halstead didn't like being spoken to like that, but, although he clamped his lips into a razor line, he said nothing, just hitched a hip on to the corner of another bed and began to roll a cigarette.

Rush Bonner was glad of the short respite: it hurt to talk and his head was thumping. But he knew if he tried to use these things to put off his explanation, Pollard would see it only as a device to give him time to make up a story.

And he sure as hell didn't need to do that!

★   ★   ★

He sheltered from the heavy rain in a kidney-shaped canyon north of the river bend, sat it out for a day and a half before deciding he might as well move on. The rain was easing now and if he read the signs right, it would have stopped by sundown.

He moved out mid-morning in the midst of a steady downpour, but nowhere near as heavy as it had been. He didn't have a strict timetable, but he knew Ben Tyson would be starting to wonder if he was going to show up at all.

And he wasn't that good a weatherman — leastways, not this far north. Back down around the Brazos he could practically have taken bets on how many minutes past the hour the rain would stop.

But here, it kept coming down — actually increased, catching him on low ground so that the horse was splashing fetlock-deep through milk-coffee water before he found the big arched cave at the base of a butte.

Obviously, it had been used before by travellers: piles of broken branches and dry brush were stacked against the rear wall, the rock blackened to the left of the pile above a wide drift of gritty grey ash. He was grateful to the unknown traveller who had been thoughtful enough to provide dry firewood for the cave's next visitor. He cooked the last of the beaver he had taken with a rawhide noose yesterday noon. It was tough but he chewed it well and was sitting picking some of the fibres from between his teeth when suddenly the cave was filled with thunder.

He saw the muzzle-flash out of the corner of his left eye and the bullet ricocheted twice from the rocky walls. By then he was sprawling on the hard floor, after diving across the fire into darkness. The gun out there in the night blasted three more times, filling the cave with snarling lead wasps.

Above their sounds, lying prone, forcing his lean body hard against the rocky floor, he heard a horse whinny, then the drumming of hoofs.

His horse!

He leapt to his feet, ran across the cave, remembering to hunch his shoulders as the roof lowered, palming up his sixgun. The night was grim, lashing rain driving into his eyes — he was hatless — and rattling off the rocks, myriad small streams spurting, mud and small rocks sliding — all mingling sounds that scrambled his hearing.

In frustration, he triggered three shots into the night, hurled a few pointless curses after the unknown horse-thief and turned back into the cave, automatically shucking out the spent shells and replacing them with fresh loads from his bullet belt.

This was a hell of fine deal! Running late to meet Ben Tyson, now without a horse. At least the damn thief had left him his saddle — which meant the man was riding bareback. Maybe the son of a bitch's own horse had died under him not far away; he'd seen the glow of the camp-fire in the cave and wasted no time getting himself a new mount, and it wasn't through lack of trying that he didn't leave a dead man behind.

But now the killer could afford to take the time to strip his dead mount of his own rig and saddle-bags, then he would simply ride off come sun-up, or maybe not even wait till then, while Bonner was left to find a way out of these hills, afoot, or drown trying to swim the flooded river, or —

'Hell, it don't matter to that lousy thief what happens to me!'

The thought made him really mad: he was less than an animal, less than nothing in the mind of the man who had stolen his roan gelding and left him afoot in the rain-lashed wilderness.

Well, the fool had made one big mistake — *two* — first was picking on Rush Bonner; the second was leaving him alive. With his guns.

★ ★ ★

It took him three days to catch up with the horse-thief.

The rain had ended before he left the cave at sun-up. It was a murky dawn, leaden clouds still tumbling across the big sky. There was lots of mud and he fell a couple of times, swearing vitriolic oaths, but he managed to keep the mud out of the barrel of his rifle. There had been no sign of deep slides in the mud, marks he didn't think the easing rain would have wiped out by now. So he figured the man hadn't gone downslope, which left across or upslope as ways to go.

It would be a battle fighting a strange horse — and bareback, too — *across* the slope with the mud sliding out underfoot. Going up and over would be hard as well, but the roan could easily carry a man up there despite the mud. And that roan was *good*, seemed to enjoy a challenge.

It wasn't such easy going for Bonner,

though, and he slid and stumbled many times before he topped-out on the ridge. Blowing hard, hands too filthy with caked mud to even try to roll a cigarette, he sat down on a rock and noticed a slight vapour rising from the landscape. The sun was beginning to heat up and that was a good sign: with a little luck and a zephyr or two out of the north, the clouds should move on or burn away, leaving one of the bluest things God ever created: the Big Sky that gave this country its nickname.

That's what happened and, late in the afternoon, Rush Bonner was rewarded for all his efforts: he saw a rider slip across the crest of the next range over. There was still enough light for him to see the reddish tint of the roan's sweaty hide. The rider was just a man in a blue shirt and dark-grey hat. The trousers looked to be brown, or maybe black, whipcord; enough to recognize the son of a bitch again.

Best of all, now he had a firm sighting and a direction.

It was a long, thirsty and hungry walk down from his mountain, and slogging up the slope of the one where he had glimpsed the thief was no better. He drank sparingly although there were still pools left from the rain: but old habits died hard. *Nurture water and food, whether it be swamp or alkali . . .* One of the first things they taught you in the cavalry. Keep a hatful for your horse and he would get you home. No horse? Eke out your supply and get yourself home.

That's what it came down to: a man had to get himself out of whatever predicament he got into, if there was no one else around to help him. Like now.

So, he had to care for himself as much as he could. Sleep was something he could use: help the body recuperate, gather strength and prepare for the next stage.

Which he hoped would be the confrontation with the man on his roan.

It was, and it happened just past high noon the following day.

He was staggering now with fatigue, even thought of abandoning the rifle because it seemed to weigh a ton and a half. He shook himself into wakefulness and, as he did so, unthinkingly stumbled out of the shadow of the timber. Next thing he was down on the ground, his head feeling as if it had been torn from his shoulders and kicked around a rocky draw by gandy dancers in hobnail boots. His hat lay a couple of yards away. He had dropped the rifle. Something wet and thick and sticky crawled across his forehead and left cheek, filling the eye socket on that side, giving him a crimson view on the world. His head rang and buzzed with noise.

Something told him not to move. *Not even a finger!*

He was fighting off oblivion. It crept up on him like some sort of assassin, rippling up from around waist level, slithering across his plexus, up his torso into his throat, choking him, so that the lack of air set his thoughts spinning wildly. He felt himself dropping away, suddenly knew only Hell waited at the bottom of that black shaft. A spark suddenly glowed in his brain, expanding, spreading heat to locked muscles and sluggish nerves. With gritted teeth and a sizzling surge of determination that cleared his throbbing brain, he forced his right eye to scan that part of the hollow he could see from his prone position.

Brush, a few saplings, some tufted grass, a gleam of water — *that* diverted him for a moment for he had a raging thirst. But then a man stood up from down there, confidently rising out of the line of brush that fringed the small waterhole. He wore a blue shirt, a grey hat and whipcord trousers, held a rifle slantwise across his chest. Bonner sucked in a hissing breath as the man began to lift the gun to his shoulder: *twice already this son of a bitch had tried to kill him! And that was twice too often.* Then a horse whinnied and briefly diverted the bushwhacker's attention.

The roan stood at the edge of the small stand of timber and the killer lowered the rifle, walked to the horse and sheathed the weapon. He mounted and rode up the slope towards where Bonner lay. He moved his left arm and shoulder a mite stiffly, Bonner thought, as he tightened his grip on the butt of his sixgun, still holstered but on the side away from the approaching killer. But, as the man drew closer, from his seat on the roan, he might be able to see Bonner's right hand . . .

He was blocky in build, switched the reins to his left hand and reached for his holstered sixgun with his right, moving very fast. *Suspicions aroused!*

Rush Bonner knew the next few seconds would decide whether he lived or died. It was a tremendous effort to fight off stampeding oblivion, to roll towards the rider, Colt sliding smoothly out of leather, fitting his hand as well as it ever did, thumb seeking the hammer spur seemingly of its own volition.

Two fast shots and the rider lifted in the stirrups, the impact of the bullets driving him clear over the roan's rump. The horse whinnied and veered away and the rider thudded to the ground, rolled and was suddenly very still.

Bonner didn't know how long he lay there with his head thundering, cheek against the warm metal of the Colt. There was no remnant of powdersmoke curling from the muzzle he focused on with his good eye, the left one still blanked out with congealing blood from his head wound.

The roan was standing to one side, ears erect, watching him, recognizing him. The shot man was on his back, making groaning, grunting sounds, but his eyes were closed and there was a lot of blood on his smashed-in chest. Some of the sounds came together and it seemed to Bonner that he was trying to say something. But Rush Bonner had his own worries and paid little atten-tion.

He lay close by, head resting on a crooked arm, and when he tried to sit up, groaned aloud at the pain driving viciously through his skull and neck. He held his head in both hands, swaying slightly. Finally, he looked up, blinking his right eye.

The horse-thief was dead now, one arm bent at the elbow, the forearm and hand raised as if in a farewell wave.

Bonner wasn't interested in him: he crawled towards his horse, grateful when it lowered its head and came closer to sniff him.

He was able to grab the trailing reins and by a series of straining efforts got to his knees, worked blood-sticky hands on to the bridle and slowly hauled himself up, the roan backing away, snorting.

He had no recollection of getting into the saddle or riding the roan out of the hollow. There was a blur of the journey but mostly everything was blank and full of pain — until he came to in the infirmary bed.

* * *

Now, he held out his empty glass and the doctor, somewhat belatedly, stepped forward and splashed some whiskey into it. Bonner held it in both hands, tossed it down his parched throat, squinting with the pain in his head.

'Easy, please!' warned the medico. 'Alcohol and head wounds do not mix well.'

Bonner grunted. 'Mostly everything after the shoot-out is a blur,' he told the group standing around his bed.

'You get some rest now,' the doctor said, a little worriedly. 'I'll give you a draught to help you sleep; you'll feel a lot better come morning.'

'Doc, hold off on the sleep, will you?' Sheriff Pollard said. 'I need to ask him some questions.'

'Not till morning, Kit,' the medico said firmly. 'He may be a lot better come morning, then again he may not. Either way, he needs sleep — now.'

Pollard looked put out, suddenly turned to Halstead. 'You stay here, Dean. I'll send Horseshoe to relieve you later. Doc, you can moan all you like, but I'm gonna have a man here all night long.'

'Surely you don't think Mr Bonner will be going anywhere, Sheriff!' Marty Rice said. 'Not in his condition.'

'Well, ma'am, I only have his word how he got in that condition. It could've been a posse bullet took him in the head, not some mystery horse-thief. I don't aim to take any chances. I'll get to bottom of things.'

Marty glanced at the pale and drawn features of Rush Bonner, smiled.

'I hope all goes well for you, Mr Bonner. I'm afraid I have to go see about my cattle and then get back to my ranch on the Stillwater. So I'll say goodbye — and good luck.' Quieter, as she briefly squeezed his shoulder, she said, 'Kit Pollard's a good man — hard but fair. He'll give you a break if he can.'

Bonner lifted a hand slightly from the sheets. 'My thanks, ma'am. I owe you my life, I reckon.'

Then the glass dropped from his limp hand as his head slumped forward and he slid down in the narrow bed.

3

Jailed

There was a man dozing in a chair against the wall, hat tilted forward over his face, when Bonner opened his eyes and focused slowly in the early light creeping into the infirmary.

He started slightly when he saw the tin star on the sleeping man's shirt pocket. Then, slowly, it came back to him and he reached up to touch the padded bandage swathing his head. He still had a headache but not as bad as it had been last night.

In fact, he felt considerably better — maybe fifty per cent of his normal self — but something stirred in him and he smiled thinly: he didn't have to let anyone *know* he was improving.

'Howdy.' The deputy thumbed back his hat, revealing a long, horselike face, feet still resting on the second chair. 'You're lookin' better, friend, than when I relieved Dean last night. Go by the name of Horseshoe.'

'Rush Bonner.' He cursed himself for answering automatically: would have been better to act confused.

Well, he would have to watch himself when the doctor came in: Bonner had a hunch that the sheriff was going to want to transfer him to the jail. The man was very suspicious. Last night, Bonner had pretended to be unconscious and heard the big deputy, Halstead, and the sheriff talking about the money they had found in those saddle-bags.

'Nearly ten thousand!' Halstead said. 'Man, too bad we can't just split it between us, Kit, but I guess too many people know about it already.'

Pollard's face was hard, deep creases between his eyes. 'That's one reason, but I'd like to think you're joshin', Dean!'

Halstead laughed. It sounded forced

to the apparently unconscious Bonner. 'Hell, 'course I am! That's money from the Miller's Ford bank robbery. Banks never give up tryin' to recover anythin' stole from 'em long as they think it's still around. Man'd be loco to try an' gyp 'em.'

'He would. Now you watch this ranny closely. I don't like his story. Too convenient and no way of checkin'.'

'Send someone to look for the man he's s'posed to've shot.'

'Sure — if the coyotes've left anythin'. Least, I've got a name now. He slipped up by mentionin' the cavalry and comin' from the Brazos country. I can tag him with that much. A few telegraph messages to the right places and by tomorrow we'll have a better picture of Mister Rush Bonner.'

The sheriff moved towards the door and Halstead said, 'We could move him to jail an' to hell with the sawbones an' his complaints.'

'Likely we'll do that. But later.'

Bonner heard the door close behind

the sheriff and then sounds of Dean Halstead arranging chairs for his comfort during his nightwatch. He drifted into a disturbed sleep, filled with old dreams of sweat and chases through darkness crawling with danger . . .

Sabres and stone tomahawks, arrows impaling screaming men, dripping scalps — then the less obvious: the stealth and the taking of sentries with a cold steel blade, a dry-gulcher's rifle blasting out of the brush along the canyon rim, squirming up to the outlaw camp and picking off the sleeping men before they could shoot back — the bar-room confrontations, gunsmoke and blood.

He woke once during the night, sweat-drenched, mouth dry, heart thudding, head bursting with fearful pressures, but the incessant buzzing and clanging in his ears was slowly diminishing. He didn't remember seeing anyone else in the room, though there was the half-memory of someone snoring.

He had reached and passed some

sort of crisis during the night. He *felt* it, a new awareness of his situation, but knowing he wasn't yet recovered enough to make any moves by himself.

He hoped the sheriff didn't get any early replies to his telegraph wires.

Doc Field was pleased, if not mildly surprised, at his condition, and Bonner knew he was going to have trouble convincing this sawbones that he wasn't as good as the man's examination suggested.

'You have mighty good powers of recovery, Mr Bonner.'

'Lots of practice, Doc.'

'I admit to some surprise, but — well, we may well try you with a short walk around the room later this afternoon.'

Bonner kept his gaunt face as blank as he could. *Hell, he hadn't expected that!* 'I dunno if I'm quite that ready, Doc.'

'Well, all the textbooks could give me plenty of arguments, but I spent some time in Europe a while back — my wife comes from there — and I watched in amazement as the medical men had patients on their feet only a day or so after having an appendix removed, or even more serious abdominal surgery.'

'I lost my appendix in the cavalry, Doc. They were cutting out an arrowhead and the sawbones figured he might's well get in some practice and took my appendix at the same time.'

Field frowned. 'Rather unethical, but — I fully understand the man's attitude. Bear with me, Mr Bonner. I'm considered something of a radical, in a small way, but I believe I will have you ready to ride in a few days.'

That was good news, providing it didn't happen while he was locked up in Pollard's jail.

He endured another day in the infirmary, a succession of grumpy deputies taking four-hour shifts to stay with him while Sheriff Pollard awaited replies to his telegraph queries. Bonner was tense: if the lawman had contacted the cavalry, it wouldn't do Bonner much good. *Damnit!* And, working out from Brazos — well, the sooner he got back on his roan and quit this place the better. With a little luck, maybe the rains had washed away a couple of telegraph poles, or the wires were down in the high winds.

He could always hope.

Dean Halstead was sitting boredly in a chair, playing solitaire on a folding table the doctor had provided, when Sheriff Pollard came back.

Bonner's belly clenched when he saw the lawman's face.

Pollard went straight to the bedside. 'You are one dangerous ranny, Bonner.'

'Not me.'

'Fort Westaway ring any bells in that bandaged head of yours?'

Dean Halstead looked up quickly from his cards. 'That's an army prison stockade, ain't it?'

Pollard ignored him, watching Bonner's face. The wounded man stared back in silence.

'Struck an officer. The man hit his

head when he fell, died some days later when everyone figured he'd recovered and gone back to duty. Never satisfactorily proved your blow caused his death, but they gave you two years in the stockade. You escaped, once, put a guard in hospital while doing it.'

Halstead pulled his chair closer to the bed. 'Well, well, well, we got us a hotshot hardcase here, eh, Kit?'

'The guard had just beaten a kid, crippled him. It was my turn next. I didn't aim to stand still for it.'

'By the time they caught you again someone else had killed that guard, because of his brutality — went in your favour. Only had another six months added to your sentence.'

'Long time ago.'

'Not so long. Only about a year since your release.'

'Seems longer.'

'Then there was a town in Utah. Recollect its name?' Bonner said nothing, his stare unwavering. 'You know where I mean. Killed two men in a barroom shootout. You wanna tell me some excuse for that?'

'They were trying to kill me.'

'Somethin' about a short deck of cards, wasn't it?'

'I forget.'

'Judas, we have us a prime one here, Kit!'

Dean Halstead sounded pleased, his eyes bright with interest. The sheriff's voice droned on.

'Then there was Deadwood, and Wichita, Omaha. Gunplay in every one. You sure move around, Bonner.'

'There're no dodgers on me, Sheriff.'

'I got your word on that, huh?'

'You have.'

'You surely won't mind if I kinda check it out for myself?'

'Whatever happened was mebbe wild and woolly but I never did any jail time worth spit.'

'Luck, pure damn luck.' Pollard's face hardened. 'But you're gonna do some jail time now, mister! I ain't about to turn you loose after that piddlin' story you told! You been caught redhanded with stolen bank money and I'm keepin' you behind bars until I look into it and satisfy myself one way or t'other how that money got in your saddle-bags.'

'They're not my saddle-bags! That's not even my rig on the roan. It was on it when I was drygulched. Belonged to the feller who stole my horse.'

'Allegedly.' Pollard turned to Halstead. 'Get the doc in here, Dean, we ain't goin' without we take this son of a bitch with us.'

'You bet, Kit!' Halstead gave Bonner a nod, flicking his eyebrows at him. 'I'll just love takin' care of you, feller.'

'I can hardly wait.'

★ ★ ★

He was behind bars, in a cell all to himself, by sundown. A couple of drunks sang desultorily two cells along.

Doc Field had cussed-out Sheriff Pollard mighty good, and the lawman had coloured deeply several times, but he remained stubborn, let the medic finish, then said, quietly, 'You can bring him any medicines you want him to have, Doc, but you check with me first and I'll take a look at 'em.'

'As if you'd know painkiller from beaver's piss!' snapped the frustrated doctor, knowing he was beaten. He heaved a heavy sigh. 'You're the law, Kit, but only until next election, if I have anything to do with it.'

'Your privilege, Doc. Now you got that old chair with iron wheels left over from the war, I believe? OK. We'll wheel Bonner on down to the jailhouse in that. See? We're gonna take real good care of him . . . '

Field shook his large head sadly, glancing at the silent, tense-looking patient. 'I'm sorry, Mr Bonner . . . '

'That's OK, Doc. Thanks for all you've done.'

One of the drunks rattled his cell door, shouting.

Dean Halstead hit the drunk's hands

with a billy. 'Just shut up, Denny, or I'll bust your goddamn head.'

That damned stubborn sheriff was going to keep on digging and, meantime, Bonner would be under surveillance by the deputies: Pollard didn't want any suspect dying in his cells. Dammit! He could be here for a mighty l-o-o-ong time.

His head was throbbing again and the ringing in his ears had reached carillon levels. He didn't feel anywhere near as spry as he had this morning back in the infirmary.

And the deputies, mostly Dean Halsted, came to check on him every hour or so, just pausing to test the door lock, rattling it loudly to wake him if he was dozing, and went away down the narrow passage, laughing, maybe dragging a billy along the other cell doors, waking the drunks from their hangovers. Halstead had a mean streak in him a mile wide.

'Hopin' there's a big price on your head, Bonner. I'm gettin' a mite tired of this job. If there's a decent bounty on you, I'll quit, and claim it for myself. Hope you've been a real bad boy. Badder they are, bigger the bounty, huh?'

Halstead went away whistling tunelessly, leaving Rush Bonner feeling dejected: this was as boring and frustrating an existence as he could remember, including the hellish stay in the Westaway stockade.

But there was nothing he could do about it. Not right now, leastways . . .

One time aroused mild interest in him, though.

Dean Halstead was being relieved by Horseshoe and, just outside the cell door, Halstead produced a large brass key from his pocket and held it up.

'Now the money's in the safe, Kit wants us to hold the key while he's out of the office — Keep it with you and when you go off duty, hang it on that special hook he put in behind the row of ledgers.'

'Why don't he just move the damn money to the bank's safe?'

'Wants the glory of findin' it, I guess. It'll be good for him come next election, and he needs all the help he can get there. Listen, if he's not in the office when you finish here, just hang the key behind the bookcase, got it? . . . OK, I'm goin'.' Dean glanced over his shoulder at Bonner. 'Too bad you'll never get to spend that dinero, Bonner!'

'In a week's time, just gimme five minutes with you. That'll be better than all the money.'

'Ooooo — ain't he scary!'

Horsehoe laughed as he put the heavy key in his pocket and Halstead sauntered away towards the front law office, ignoring the pleas of one of the recovering drunks to be allowed to empty the over-flowing slop-bucket.

Two days later, Bonner felt like kicking down the stone walls of the cell: he was restless now his strength was returning and he wanted out.

Doc Field had made sure he was given good meals and personally administered his medicines. He could see how well Bonner had progressed and enthused about it within hearing of the lawmen. Bonner said quietly,

'Be obliged if you kind of played down how fit I'm s'posed to be, Doc.' The medic frowned, puzzled. 'Mebbe we could just keep it between you and me.'

Field lifted his head quickly. 'Oh! Damn me for an old fool! I didn't realize I was making things more difficult for you. Are you treated more harshly because they see you improving so quickly?'

It wasn't exactly what Bonner had meant but it would do. 'They tend to be a mite rougher.'

Field nodded, putting a finger across his lips. 'Mr Bonner, you're doing tolerably well, but you have a long way to go yet, I'm afraid. You get as much rest as you can.'

Dean Halstead and Horseshoe were

44

both in the passage and heard the doctor clearly. A strange look passed between them and then Dean opened the door and let the doctor out. Horsehoe escorted Field down the passage while Halstead leaned against the wall opposite the doors, rolling a cigarette. There were no other prisoners in the cellblock now. 'Kit's had some more wires about you.'

'When's he turning me loose?'

Dean laughed harshly, licked his cigarette paper, twisted it into shape. 'You sure are Mr Hopeful. From what I gather, you're on the run from a warrant down in Cochise County, coupla years old.'

'News to me. Couple of years ago, I was still in the stockade.'

'Which is maybe how come they missed pickin' you up — didn't know you were there. Or you were usin' a different name . . .'

There was a query there but Bonner's face remained blank and Halstead grinned, blew a plume of smoke through the bars and began to walk away.

'You been a ba-a-d boy, Bonner, I'm happy to say. You got several thousand bucks ridin' on your head.'

Bonner gripped the bars, feeling a rush of dizziness.

'You're loco! There's no warrant out on me!'

'Ask Kit!' Halstead's laughter drifted down the passage and, swearing to himself, Bonner sat down on the bunk, absently fingering the small patch of cotton pad which was all that covered his headwound now.

Someone was setting him up for something!

He didn't know what, but there was nothing he could do about it, locked up in here.

★ ★ ★

Dean Halstead himself collected the supper dishes making Bonner lie down on his face on the bunk while he did so. Holding the tray in one hand, fumbling at the door where the keys dangled in the lock with the other, the deputy kept his hard stare on the prisoner.

'Sheriff tell you about that Cochise County warrant yet?'

'No — but you tell him I want to see him.'

'Tell him yourself — '

'*Dean! Dean!*'

Still fumbling at the door, Halstead snapped his head up as Horseshoe came hurrying down the passage. 'The hell're you yellin' at?'

'Christ! You better come quick! Fuzz Carmody's been on that moonshine of his again and he's wreckin' the saloon, threw Mitch Wallis through the street window.'

'I got jail duty. Go tell the sheriff.'

'He's off seein' that dancehall gal he's been sparkin'. Judas, Dean, Fuzz's got that damn big Bowie and half the drinkers're crammed into a corner, too scared to move! There's gonna be bloody murder done if — '

'Goddamnit! All right, *all right*! I'll come.'

Halstead pulled the door closed, juggling the tray of dishes, turned to Horsehoe who was jumping from one foot to the other. 'Well, for Chris'sakes, get back down there and try to keep Fuzz from cuttin' someone up! I'll be there soon as I get a sawn-off from the office.'

He swore savagely as he dropped the tray and dishes shattered. The deputy kicked them aside angrily and then hurried away down the dim passage, leaving the mess.

Bonner sat up on the bunk. 'Gonna be a lively night in the ol' town tonight,' he observed, wishing he had had time to finish that cup of coffee before Halstead had stormed in and snatched the tray away from him.

His gaze went to the clutter on the floor of the passage and he saw the cup was smashed anyway, dark coffee spilled and crawling under the cell bars, and . . .

He stiffened, staring.

The cell door was open about six inches.

In all his fumbling and yelling, Dean Halstead couldn't have turned the key properly so the lock hadn't gone completely home.

Bonner ran a tongue around suddenly dry lips.

4

Rush Away

The saloon was in uproar.

Broken glass was all over the boardwalk along the front. One batwing hung by a single hinge, some slats broken — later it was established this was where Fuzz Carmody had entered, crashing through like a bear with a bee stuck in his nostrils. Tables were overturned. Two chairs were splintered. Three men were stretched out unconscious in the scuffed and wet sawdust.

A tight bunch of ex-drinkers, mostly townsmen and so unarmed, were pressing back into one corner at the end of the bar. The 'keep was sitting on a stool, holding a soiled bar towel to a bleeding face. There was no sign of the man he hired as helper on busy nights.

In front of the bar there was a big

50

fellow in stained buckskins, fringed shirt hanging outside his trousers, tree-trunk legs spread. The smoky lanterns reflected from the long, wide blade of the Bowie knife he waved in one huge fist. Long greasy hair spilled across a dirt-caked, stubbled face, eyes glittering in deep sockets.

'I want Melody!' the big one roared, waving the knife carelessly, causing the already tight-knit bunch to move even closer together.

The barkeep, face bloody and mangled, lowered the stained towel a few inches. His words were slurred because of a swollen mouth and several broken teeth.

'I keep tellin' you, Fuzz, she — ain't — here! She ain't worked here in six months!'

The blade flashed in a deadly arc and the 'keep reared back hard enough to slam into the lower shelves, spilling bottles to the floor where they shattered.

'Goddammit! You're still causin' damage, Fuzz! You ain't never gonna be able to pay for all this!'

'I ain't payin' for nothin'.' Fuzz feinted towards the crowd with the huge knife and there was a mad scramble and yells of alarm.

'Ain't anyone wearin' a gun, for Chris'sakes?' someone called.

And then the batwings slammed back, the damaged one falling off completely with a clatter.

'About goddamn time!' roared the barkeep, sidling out from the end of the bar now, past Fuzz who had turned to see who had come in. 'Kill the son of a bitch! Give him both barrels, Dean!'

Dean Halstead ignored the barkeep and motioned for Horseshoe to move out to the side. He brought up the sawn-off shotgun and cocked both hammers.

The men jam-packed into the corner all dropped to the floor, rolling and fighting for places away from the possible spread of buckshot.

But the deputy didn't fire. Carmody, swaying on his big bare feet with their horny nails protruding from crusted mountain dirt, snarled like an animal, lifting the Bowie knife threateningly.

'That the way you want it, Fuzz?' The shotgun barrels jerked a little. 'You take one step and I'll blow you in half.'

'I just wanna see Melody!'

'You know damn well she ran out with that drummer that sold ladies' corsets last summer. Why the hell you keep lookin' for her? She ain't gonna come back here to the likes of you when she can have herself a high ol' time with that drummer. He'll dump her eventually but till then they — '

'*You shut up!*'

'Sure, Fuzz, I can do that, but it won't change nothin'. Now, you gonna drop that knife or . . . '

Dean Halstead tilted the gun barrels and dropped the left-hand hammer. There were yells of alarm and curses and a lot of movement among the squirming men as laths and bits of plaster and part of the wagonwheel chandelier came crashing to the floor in the wake of the sudden thunder.

Fuzz jumped back, lifting his knife arm across his face in an instinctive protective gesture.

Halstead signed to Horseshoe and they rushed in while Fuzz was partially blinded by his own arm and off-balance. The shotgun thudded across Fuzz's skull from the left and Horseshoe's carbine barrel bounced off the thick bone from the right.

Both deputies stepped back hurriedly as the man merely turned his head to look at them, fresh blood pouring down over his craggy, bewhiskered face.

'Aw, hell!' gasped Horseshoe getting ready to run.

Then Fuzz Carmody's arm shot out and grabbed the deputy's arm, shaking him. 'You done it! You was the one tol' me Melody was back!'

'You're loco!' Horseshoe yelled, turning a white, terrified face towards Halstead. 'Shoot him, Dean! No! Don't — you'll cut me in two as well.'

'Why you lie to me about Melody!?'

The Bowie swung up, then down towards Horsehoe's ghastly face as he struggled and started to scream. But Dean Halstead stepped around the mountain man's huge bulk, this time used both hands to swing the shotgun, and smashed it across the back of Fuzz's head. Wild hair flew around his face, leaves, twigs and other debris, including dead insects, spilled from it. Fuzz snarled at Dean, making him jump back.

'Hey, Dean, I never — Why you . . . do . . . that . . . ?'

His thick legs suddenly folded and he dragged Horseshoe to the floor with him as he collapsed.

The collective sigh in the bar room was like the first gust of a mid-summer storm.

Horseshoe staggered up and immediately kicked the unconscious big man twice in the side. Halstead pulled him back.

'He's out to it.' He looked around at the relieved and sweating drinkers. 'Need a couple men to carry Fuzz down to the cells — before he comes to.'

'More like a coupla dozen!'

'And a goddamn wagon team! He weighs more'n a keg of tallow!'

'Come on,' Halstead said impatiently. 'Horsehoe an' me put him down. Six of you can handle him easy.'

'An' what're you an' Horseshoe gonna do?'

'I'm goin' on ahead and move some furniture so's you can get that man-mountain through the office — I'll get a cell ready, too. Horseshoe'll walk behind and see he don't come round and throw you up on the roof of the Courthouse as you go by.'

The group didn't like considering the possibility of that happening. Only after Halstead had cuffed Fuzz's huge hands behind him, did half-a-dozen reluctant 'volunteers' strain and puff as they lifted Carmody, staggering past the single batwing, starting the lumbering journey to the jailhouse.

Dean Halstead hurried on ahead.

It was several minutes before the group appeared outside the law offices and, as they struggled at the foot of the landing steps, Dean appeared in the doorway, a lamp burning behind him now. They couldn't see his face too well but they heard the strain in his voice as he called to Horseshoe.

'Get in here! Quick!'

Puzzled, Horsehoe frowned, pushed past the panting group with their burden and hurried up the steps. Dean reached quickly and pulled him inside.

'What's wrong, Dean . . . ? Oh, sweet Jesus!'

Outside, the panting men stopped abruptly. They let Fuzz fall and the landing shook as they stepped over him and crammed into the front office. Their eyes popped as they stared at the scene before them.

Sheriff Kit Pollard was on the floor beside his desk lying face up, a hunting knife buried to the hilt in his chest. Blood was still oozing and pooling on the floor beneath him.

'Someone's killed the sheriff!' one man in front called back to the others who were straining to see.

'And not long ago,' Dean Halstead said grimly. 'Safe's open, too, and the money's gone.'

'Gun cabinet's been busted open,' observed Horsehoe gesturing to the splintered door of the mahogany cupboard.

'Hell almighty!' Halstead pointed to the safe door: the brass key was in the lock and the bookshelf it had been hidden behind was knocked askew, some of the ledgers scattered on the floor. 'Someone knew where to look for the key. Horseshoe, go check the cells!'

The deputy pushed through the crowding men who were all talking at once, ran out into the cell-block passage. Before he was halfway along, he yelled, 'There's a door hangin' open. Last cell in the block — Bonner's busted out!'

In the front office, Dean Halstead's face hardened.

'Well, we know who done all this then!

He knew about the key. I remember handin' it to Horseshoe outside his cell when we were changin' shifts. *Goddamn!*' He heaved a sigh. 'All right, you men, go tell your wives and families you're ridin' on a posse! An' not to expect you home anytime soon: we won't be comin' back till we get this son of a bitch. We leave in twenty minutes!'

★   ★   ★

Rush Bonner wasn't as fit as he had figured.

He had to cling to the saddlehorn, reins twisted around one wrist, so as to keep from swaying like a paper lantern at a hoedown. Thank God the horse was his own and knew the feel of him.

He had been mighty surprised and pleased to find the roan in the small stables behind the law office. He didn't know whose saddle he had grabbed in the dark and thrown across the roan, but that didn't matter.

Main thing was he was free.

He had padded along the dark passage after slipping out of his cell, down to the empty front office, still not fully believing that he was on his way to freedom.

No lights: there were still too many folk on the streets. So he groped his way to the gun cupboard where he had seen Pollard stow his guns when first brought here. It was locked, as was to be expected. He found a heavy-bladed hunting knife in a top drawer of the desk and prised the hasp out of the wood, working well enough in the darkness. He tossed the knife carelessly on to the desk, wrenched open the cupboard door, wood splintering, the sound making him wince. His sixgun rig was there, and several other weapons. He buckled on his Colt then took a rifle from the rack. He wasn't sure if it was his but . . . *who cared!*

Snatching up a couple of cartons of shells, heart pounding, head spinning, he was about to start back down the passage when the street door opened.

Stiff as a flagpole, he pressed back into the heavy shadows against the wall. Dim light washed across the desk, briefly reflecting from the blade of the hunting knife.

The newcomer entered, humming softly to himself, then stopped dead in his tracks as he saw the open gun cabinet with its splintered door. Bonner caught a whiff of cheap perfume and whiskey, knew at once who it was.

Sheriff Kit Pollard, returning from a visit to his dancehall girl.

The lawman must have heard Bonner's sharp indrawing of breath, turned quickly towards the sound in the shadows, reaching for his gun . . .

★   ★   ★

Now, riding through the night, Bonner felt his throat constrict at the memory of that brief encounter, lifted his face to catch some of the breeze made by the roan's passage.

By now he was well clear of town: the

further away the better! He had avoided the twin arched bridges across Beaverhead Creek and ridden upstream until he found a place to cross. The horse had to swim and the cold water brought him properly awake.

But he still felt kind of weak and the weight of his gunbelt around his waist was surprisingly heavy. He couldn't remember ever noticing it before, during all the years he had carried a sixgun.

So, it was something to think about: in the confines of the cell, with the bunk available for recuperative sleep twenty-four hours a day, reasonable grub and Doc Fields' attention and medicines, he had felt ready to kick his way out and into the world at large.

Just as well Halstead fumbled that damn door lock! He'd never have gotten free without that providential mistake by the big deputy.

But now, after what were essentially mild exertions, he was already breathless, light-headed, his heart hammering:

and he had that bitter, dry, raspy taste of apprehension — if not downright fear — like he had swallowed a handful of alkali.

He knew a posse would be coming — and quickly.

The night wind was cool, though, and he welcomed it fanning his hot face, helping him to think a bit more clearly. But there was a little dampness in it, too. Which could mean more rain. *That* wouldn't hurt any: it would help cover his tracks.

He had no real plan — the breakout had come too suddenly for that: he had had to act *right* then or lose the chance.

The dark and faraway hills towering across the night sky, some with permanent snow caps, were both a barrier and his salvation. He wasn't sure just what lay behind them, more mountains or lots of wide-open country. Probably dotted with a few small towns, which the posse would be sure to check.

He needed to find a pass, a way through the Bitterroots that would lead him to Ben Tyson's country. But could he risk going there now? All the lawmen knew he was on his way to see Tyson; he had told them early on. They could soon track Ben down, even in that wide-open country far beyond the Bitterroots.

Dammit! He needed to put all the miles he could between himself and the posse, but the way he felt, he knew he was going to have to find some place to hole-up for a spell.

He had to face up to it: he wasn't as tough as he thought. His head was throbbing again, the wound pounding like an Indian drum. His entire body was a'tremble.

There was nothing else for it: back there, the lights of the town were still in sight, just a few dull pinpoints, but *there*. He had to find some place to stop pretty damn soon or the posse would simply ride up and find him sprawled across the trail, out cold with fatigue, the roan cropping grass nearby.

Easy pickings.

5

Big Mountain

Dean Halstead was a trifle shaken: there were twenty men in the posse and he could have had at least a dozen more. He hadn't figured on handling that many.

It was a surprise to know Kit Pollard had been so popular, with the ordinary folk anyway, but not so much with the business faction. Pollard had always ignored approaches by them for things he saw as adding value — and prices — to their business, but only at the expense of ordinary townsfolk of whom he was one. And he didn't like the way they looked down their noses at him because of his interest in a half-breed dancehall girl.

He was impartial invoking the law and the town ordinance, refused many a bribe, in cash or kind, to go easy on a member of some rich family who broke a rule.

'You're one of the richest men in town,' he might tell the man trying his luck. 'You got money enough to pay the fine — an' it could go higher, with the possibility of a jail term added, if you keep tryin' to bribe me.'

That kind of story went down well with the townsfolk although they all knew the council, composed mostly of business people, would do their best to undermine Pollard's re-election. He was stubborn, hard, but still fair in the eyes of the regular folk — there were already plans afoot to bring in kinfolk from all over the county on election day to ensure Kit's re-election. He had had that rare thing in a frontier sheriff — integrity.

Dean Halstead had been aiming to contest the sheriff's job: he had been approached quietly by representatives of the council, feeling him out. He was willing to listen and the prospect of his bank balance growing at a fast clip once he was in office definitely influenced his decision . . . but none of that mattered now.

Although he hadn't figured on bossing such a large posse, it did mean Rush Bonner was going to have one hell of a tough time trying to escape. These men were out for blood. If their drive began to flag, Dean knew he only had to mention the Miller's Ford bank's reward for the return of the money to rejuvenate their interest.

That's what would run Bonner to ground in the end, hopefully in a blazing shoot-out, with Bonner dead when the gunsmoke cleared.

Dean felt he couldn't lose . . .

Billy-Bob Cougar rode into the camp as the red-eyed posse men gathered around Dean, awaiting orders for the day. He was the half-breed brother of the dancehall girl, Winnie Water-Flower, that Kit Pollard had been 'interested' in.

When hearing of Kit's murder, after

a lot of tears she had sent for her brother. He was the worse for wear, having spent most of the night with bucks from the reservation, drinking homemade *tiswin*.

Flower's sloe eyes regarded him with contempt and she snapped at him in rapid Lakota. Billy-Bob managed to look ashamed, but only so she would stop shouting at him — the top of his head rose and fell with every loud insult.

She was a fine-looking woman, slim and golden, raven-haired, with dark, flashing eyes, but she looked mighty ugly to him now as she cussed him out — *but good*.

'Kit has been killed by that bank robber. You join the posse — *and you find him!* Bring me his ears.'

Billy-Bob looked sullen. 'I got to meet my frien's.'

'You do and I kill you, Billy-Bob Cougar! You know I mean it. Now go. Ride with Halstead and find that murderer.'

Tears rolled down her dusky face, but she steadied herself, dark eyes boring into the man.

'Kit wanted to marry me! He was a good man — '

'An' what you give him in return, eh?'

Her hand stung his rough cheek and shook his eyeballs in their sockets. He made no attempt to strike her back, although he wanted to.

'You should have been named Billy The Pig! Kit was eager to marry me, but I said no, because it would ruin his career.' Her lip curled in a sneer. 'These men who would ruin him if he did marry me — they like to come see me dance, show my body, but I am not good enough to be respectable like their wives and sweethearts!' Her bosom heaved with emotion and Billy waited, uninterested, but trapped. Her sweet voice hardened. 'You do what I say! I am elder, your only family. You obey or I sing of all your sins to the Night Spirit . . . '

Billy-Bob paled. He might be a waster, drinking and whoring with the reservation bucks, rolling drunks behind the saloon, but he still held abject fears of the afterlife and the inevitable accounting of his sins before the Great Spirit. Deep down, he held respect for his older sister — if somewhat reluctantly — because of his tribal upbringing.

So he turned his battered hat brim through his hands and nodded. 'I find him — I bring you his ears.'

'Yes.'

★ ★ ★

He had joined the posse and been accepted readily by Dean for the man was known to be an excellent tracker — if you could keep him sober. He was a drinking pard of Fuzz Carmody's and when the two of them were on the moonshine, well, Dean Halstead was ready to shoot the 'breed if he tried anything like that now.

70

'What you find, Billy?' he saw the 'breed's nostrils twitch at the smell of cooking food — bacon, corncakes and beans — even heard the man's belly growl. 'You can eat before we hit the trail.'

Halstead's words brought a few heads snapping up. One of the townsmen, named Tab Hemming, a foreman at Delman's freight yard, said, 'He can eat on the run, dammit. Every minute counts.'

'Billy's been out all night trackin' while you been sleepin'. He's earned a decent meal. You're closest, Tab. Stack him a platter while he reports to me.'

'I don't wait on no damn 'breed.'

Dean sighed. 'He's gonna lead us to Bonner, dammit!'

'Not if we don't get ridin'!' another man snapped.

Dean turned as Billy-Bob spoke.

'I think he went into the Bitterroots.'

'Hell almighty!' Hemming exclaimed in disgust. 'A blind man could figure that!'

71

Billy-Bob lowered his eyes, not in reprimand, but to hide the flare of hatred he felt for most of these white men. Kit Pollard had been all right, but Dean and these others . . . they only used him when it suited. Mostly he was treated like a pariah.

'Tracks wanderin' all over,' he said sullenly. 'I think he looks for a way across — or through. He dunno this land.'

Dean nodded. 'Could be right. All the better for us. OK, mount up, men. We'll ride to the foothills and spread out.'

'Spread out? Hell, Dean, the 'breed should take us to where he found the tracks and — ' Hemming began.

'There's a lot of us,' cut in the deputy, frowning. 'We spread out, we can cover a lot more ground. Me an' Billy-Bob'll ride to where he found the tracks and figure things from there while the rest of you look for more sign. It'll save time in the long run.'

There were growls and complaints

and Dean knew they were all thinking about the reward now. Sure, they were still riled about Kit's murder, but it was obvious every man there wanted to be in on the kill so he could claim a piece of the reward.

'Let's get movin', anyway, or we might's well start cookin' the noon meal,' someone growled.

Billy-Bob jumped from his saddle and quickly spilled the now-burned corncakes and bacon on to a tin platter, covered them with a couple of spoonfuls of beans and began to eat noisily.

'I don't feel like sharin' no reward with that trash!' Hemming opined loud enough for Billy to hear. But the 'breed didn't raise his head, only slurped more loudly.

'Be glad he's with us,' Horsehoe said, tightening his cinchstrap. 'He's the best tracker around — only better one is Fuzz. Someone like to go let him outa jail an' bring him here?'

There were no takers and no more talk. Billy-Bob was ready to ride as soon as the posse, wiping bean gravy from his greasy fingers on his clothes. Hemming spat disgustedly.

Dean broke the posse into three, seven men in each group, Horseshoe leading one, Hemming another, and Dean himself the third — with Billy-Bob Cougar.

He gestured to the towering grey range. 'Tab, you take your bunch, sweep in from the west, go up but converge on that column of boulders near the top; they call 'em Red Cloud's Arrow. Horseshoe, you come in from the east to the same place. The Arrow's our rendezvous for sundown.'

'Hell! If that 'breed's as good as you say, we oughta have Bonner before then!'

'With some luck, Tab, yeah, we might, but if we don't, them boulders is where we meet. I'll lead my group dead centre on the range.'

Hemming wasn't happy and several of the others were the same. 'I don't see why we can't go to where Billy found them tracks and spread out from there.

Makes more sense to me. We'll have the son of a bitch by sundown that way.'

Others murmured agreement: it did seem like Dean Halstead was wasting a lot of time and giving everyone a lot of unnecessary hard riding.

'Goddamnit! We do it like I say!' snapped Dean, fed-up with all this questioning of his authority. 'Comin' in from three sides, we're gonna corner Bonner. Now get movin'.'

The groups started to head in the directions Dean had indicated, but more than one man complained that while Dean's theory might be all right, it was all right only as long as Bonner didn't find the pass ahead of them and slip through to the Big Sky Country beyond.

Then it could take weeks to run him down.

⋆ ⋆ ⋆

It was full daylight and Bonner was hungry.

There was no food in the saddle-bags that had been with the saddle he had taken, only an old shirt in one and nothing in the other. He had no canteen and would have to find water.

The fact that he had slept so long, well past sun-up bothered him: he had intended to start up the mountain before then. He must have needed that sleep though: taking stock of himself, he realized that, although he was stiff from sleeping on the crude bed of green boughs he had made against the canted boulder, he felt better.

There was a new clarity in his thinking and his observations. He *wanted* to be on the trail now, whereas yesterday he'd regarded it as an annoying necessity and had forced himself although he would rather have rested. His arms and shoulders were stiff. He moved them several times, straightening and pressing his hands against the small of his back. Yes, he was much improved, although the wound on the top of his head was still sore. The gunrig dragged at his waist and he adjusted the belt up one notch and settled it more comfortably. Pausing, he suddenly snatched at the weapon, hand filling smoothly with the butt, wrist taking the weight and instinctively adjusting to the balance, thumb already resting on the hammer spur — all without conscious thought.

Bonner smiled faintly. *He was much improved!*

The ease with which he drew the Colt added to his feeling of well-being. His growling belly did nothing for it. On a rock twenty feet away, he saw a squirrel calmly eating some sort of nut or root. One shot and his hunger would be taken care of: one shot, and he would have a damn posse on his neck!

'Go on! Git outa here!' He waved his arms as he yelled and the squirrel disappeared in an instant. He half-smiled. 'Your lucky day, you little son of a bitch.'

The roan had been cropping grass and was ready for riding, though no doubt it would appreciate a drink. Bonner had left him saddled all night, just with a loosened cinchstrap, which he tightened firmly now. The horse turned its head, snorted quietly, and nudged his arm. He stroked the muzzle and tweaked one ear, then led it to a rock, stood on top, and eased himself into the saddle.

Looking up the steep slope, he had the strange feeling that the mountain was toppling down on him, but it was only the fluffy white clouds moving across the deep-blue sky. He slid the Winchester from the scabbard, rode out of the small stand of timber, feeling his body tense as he left cover behind.

There was a ledge almost directly above his postition, and, seeing that there was no other vantage point at that level on this particular slope, he eased the roan up. It was a stiff climb and the horse grunted a lot, but when there, he moved as close to the rockface as he could, hunting the deepest shadow.

His good feeling deserted him in the

snap of a finger.

There was the damn posse! To the left, a whole bunch of riders — five — six! One man was dismounted and studying the ground. *Had he ridden across that particular stretch?* He didn't think so. *But they were too blamed close.*

Now he had his problems: if he moved off this ledge, they would see him, for sure. There was only open slope above, almost to the crest, before a slushy line of cap snow began. And *that* wouldn't offer any cover, only silhouette him more easily.

If he stayed put? He might get away with it, but the way those men were working across the slope, they were going to stumble on the little nook he had made for himself last night. Just one sight of those broken boughs he had shaped roughly like a bed and they would know they were on the right trail.

He fingered the rifle. It would be easy to pick them off, *or their mounts*!

Bonner dismounted, placed a heavy

rock on the rein ends to temporarily anchor the roan, and crawled to the edge, levering a shell into the rifle. He didn't like having to shoot healthy horses but his own health and well-being depended on breaking up those men below.

They were likely only a small part of the main posse and the gunfire would bring the others.

The old proverbial 'between a rock and a hard place'!

Well, he'd been there before, many times, but he felt disadvantaged here. So, *make your move quickly, get things going, see how they were going to turn out for better or worse?*

He picked the tracker first: the man had his head lowered over a clod of earth, was scratching with his fingers peering closely when Bonner fired his first shot.

The clod exploded into the man's face and he heard the wild yell through the echoing gunshot. The man reared back, clawing at his eyes, lost his footing and tumbled down to the still mounted men, sliding against the legs of one horse. There was immediate disorder as the horse reared, and threw its unprepared rider into the next man. More tangled, men and horses, as Bonner's rifle crashed twice more. A horse went down beneath another rider and the two still mounted spurred hurriedly for cover. He hastened them along with two more shots, put another bullet between the downed men. The blinded one yelled hoarsely and staggered away from the group. The other two leapt and plunged wildly down the slope in the wake of the mounted men.

It was much better than Bonner had expected and he mounted the roan swiftly, spurred off the ledge and around behind the standing rock above it. He was ready to make his run up the open slope when he noticed the big, flat rock balanced on the very edge above the ledge he had just quit.

The roan sensed his urgency, was eager to go, but suddenly Bonner slid from the saddle, ran to the balanced rock. Just leaning hard against it made it teeter a little. Below, the men were recovering and rifles hammered, bullets whining and ricocheting from the ledge itself. Seemed they hadn't seen him make his exit during their panic.

He dropped the rifle, pressed hands and shoulder against the balanced rock, braced his boots against irregularities on the surface of the rock underfoot, and strained. Pain filled his skull as blood suffused his brain with the effort and he thought he was going to pass out, ears roaring, but he strained, using his legs for power, as well as his upper body.

The boulder teetered again, but, better than that, the base skidded across some gravel underneath with a crunching sound — and the boulder slid past the edge. Gasping, legs trembling with effort, he yelled with one mighty effort and — the boulder fell, crashing on to the ledge below, splintering it with a sound that momentarily drowned the gunfire. Rock shards hummed and flew into the air and, briefly, the slope was screened by a cloud of dust.

He was lying prone now, heart hammering, vision blurred, whole body feeling as if it had been squeezed in some giant vice. The dust boiled up past him and he saw the disruption and chaos he had caused below. The men and the mounts still able to, had scattered across the torn-up face of the slope. The boulder was rampaging on, smashing through brush, gouging an earth-spewing path, unstoppable.

Despite his distress, he smiled. *Round one to me!*

6

Relentless

Above the slushline, the snow was white and clean and cold. He dismounted and threw his weight on the reins, helping the roan through belly-deep snow, finally making it over the crest.

Before sliding over, he glanced down the other face of the mountain. There was a big scar on the slope from the boulder and collapsed ledge. The posse men were gathered at the edge of broken trees and he counted six, but only four horses. Moving his gaze he saw the two carcasses lying on the slope above the group.

It was clear they were reluctant to start up again, in case he was waiting to pick them off.

Hold that thought, he told them silently. He crammed a handful of snow into his dry and raspy mouth and sucked in a sharp breath at its coldness. It ran through his teeth like a bolt of lightning but he chewed and crunched and swallowed. It tended to freeze his gullet but it was wet and offered relief from his thirst.

He filled his hat with snow, pummelled and squeezed it into a sloppy mush and offered it to the roan which licked and sucked it up gratefully. There was a trickle of clear-water run-off from melting snow and he cupped his hands, several times, and swallowed. Pure and satisfying.

One more glance over the crest to make sure the posse men were still arguing about coming after him — they were — and he led the horse through the cap snow, both floundering until they were clear and slogging through slush that eventually gave way to hard-packed soil.

He climbed into the saddle and lost some time choosing a zigzag path down the mountain.

A vast land lay beyond, rolling hills and timbered slopes, shadowy gulches, a crumbling red butte that looked as if it might hide a network of canyons — which meant rockpools. It was closer than the green hills where he saw a meandering narrow line of dark trees, possibly marking the course of a creek across a flat area between the hills.

Water would not be a problem — except he still had nothing to carry it in — but food might be harder. He daren't use his guns for the posse would be gathering by now, combining, planning, pursuing him relentlessly.

He knew other methods of procuring wild food — traps, nooses, deadfalls — but they all took time to prepare. And it was usually necessary to wait until an animal or bird overcame its timidity before becoming a victim.

Putting distance between himself and the posse was the main thing right now.

He made for the butte: could be some squirrels or jack-rabbits in there, but he would likely have to hunt them at night and there would be a very real risk of twisting an ankle or breaking a leg or arm. Still, hunger would not be denied completely and if he had to chance delay or minor injury so as to procure food, he would.

He rode carefully, watching behind as well as forward. He checked the skyline of the mountain he was leaving but so far hadn't seen any riders topping-out on the crest. He urged the roan on, wanting to get under cover before he was spotted.

The sun enveloped his body in heat and the sweat poured from him — fluid his body could not afford to lose. But there was no option: ride or die.

It was an hour, maybe two, after noon before he rode into the creeping black shadow of the butte. Immediately, he felt the coolness and the roan gave a whinny or two to show it appreciated the change.

He found a craggy, zigzagging cutting that led him between high stone walls and into an open area with piles of gravelly sand telling him right away there would be water here caught in the hollows. Telltale scour marks in the soft rock gave him a direction and led him to an oblong dark pool nestling beneath a rock overhang.

Both man and animal buried their faces in the cool still water. Bonner had to force himself to cease drinking. He worried about the roan over-indulging but its instincts cut in; it drank deeply, then stepped back, shaking its head, droplets flying, as it whinnied again in pleasure.

Carefully searching the edges of the sand drift pile, he found some animal tracks — looked like a jack-rabbit — and he searched for a nearby bush. They usually spent the day in their nests or 'forms' which they hollowed out at the bases of bushes, close to their water supply.

He saw the form but not the animal and deliberately stayed away. He would wait for nightfall — as long as the posse didn't arrive before then. He had no knife, wishing briefly for that big hunter that had been lying on Kit Pollard's desk — but he broke off a bough about three feet long, stripped it of leaves and began to rub one end on the rock. It was hot, thirsty work but the splintered end gradually took on the shape of a point. It wasn't very sharp but with any luck he might be able to swipe the rabbit and break its neck, rather than have to try to stab it.

'You show the patience of an Indian.'

Bonner jumped at the sound of the voice behind, dropped the stick and, still hunkered down, turned, right hand whipping to his Colt. But he froze when he saw the man in dirty buckskins standing there, covering him with a rifle.

'You move quietly as a snake,' Bonner countered, heart hammering, not seeing the man properly because of the angle of the sun.

'As a cougar,' the man corrected. 'Billy-Bob Cougar.'

Carefully, Bonner stood, holding his

hands well out from his sides. The rifle muzzle rose with him. 'You the tracker?'

Billy-Bob nodded once. 'You're pretty good, but comin' here was too obvious.' His head jerked as he indicated the canyon.

'No choice. Needed water. And grub.'

'Yeah, they said you were without food or a canteen. You done good, though, seein' as you been head-shot.'

Bonner gestured to the rifle. 'Not good enough.'

'Nah, I ain't gonna use the rifle on you. That'd bring them other fools a'runnin' an' I don't aim to share any bounty with them. I'm gonna stick a knife in you like you done to Sheriff Kit, then use it to cut your ears off to take back to my sister.'

Rush Bonner stared, deep creases between his eyes. 'I never knifed the sheriff or anyone else.'

Billy-Bob Cougar arched his thin black eyebrows. 'Someone stuck a damn big huntin' knife in Kit's heart

— had to be you. You busted outa your cell, took your guns, and the money from the safe. Looks like the sheriff walked in on you.'

Bonner was mighty tense now, his hands clenched into fists. He saw the increased wariness in the 'breed.

'Yeah, Pollard walked in on me just as I was about to go. He reached for his Colt but I didn't want any gunfire to bring half the town down on me, so I swiped him across the head with my rifle barrel. Caught him good — he dropped like a poled steer. I got outa there via the rear door. The safe was locked when I left.'

Billy-Bob looked confused. 'Halstead said you knew where the key was.'

'How the hell would I know that? Wait! Halstead gave the key to Horse-hoe when they were changing shifts, right outside my cell, told him where to hide it behind some books — '

The 'breed was smiling crookedly now. 'See?'

'But I never even thought about it, or

that stolen money they found on me! All I wanted to do was get out of there before Halstead and Horseshoe came back.'

'Sure.'

'Well, I ain't gonna stand here and try to convince you. I see you've already made up your mind I'm your man.'

'Mebbe — mebbe not. Don't matter. Flower thinks you killed Kit and she wants your ears and I'm gonna give 'em to her. And claim the reward on you. Don't matter to me if you're guilty or not. You just one more white man who'd kick my ass if he got the chance.' He grinned. 'But you gonna make me rich, feller!'

'The hell I am!'

Bonner was ready for him, sensing he was going to make a move now, and because he didn't want to shoot and bring in others who would claim a share of the bounty, Billy-Bob wouldn't pull the trigger.

So Billy-Bob lunged forward, stabbing at Bonner's midriff with the rifle barrel.

Bonner stepped aside swiftly, pivoting, one hand snatching the rifle, his right leg coming around with the force of his turning body behind it. The boot caught Cougar mid-thigh and the man yelled in surprise as his leg gave way under him and he fell to one knee.

Bonner yanked hard on the rifle. Billy-Bob tightened his grip and was pulled forward, further off-balance. His face was just in the right position for Bonner's rising knee. The nose crunched and blood spurted as the 'breed was hurled back, so fast that Bonner missed hitting his skull with the rifle barrel.

The 'breed snatched a knife from his belt sheath and slashed. The tip caught the back of Bonner's hand and he dropped the gun. Then Cougar was surging up and lunging at him with the glinting blade.

Rush Bonner leapt back, arms flung wide, as the tip hissed across his shirtfront, slashing the cloth and barely missing his flesh. The 'breed was an experienced knife-fighter and he set his feet, one well in front of the other, which was slightly bent for stability, weaved his upper body, then lunged again.

To his surprise, Bonner wasn't where he was supposed to be and then a thudding crack across the back of Billy's neck drove him into a forward stumble. Bonner kicked him in the body as he fell and the knife dropped silently into the sand drift. Billy-Bob was angry that he was being bested by this white man and his rage was his undoing.

He scooped up a handful of coarse sand and flung it at Bonner's head. The fugitive leapt to the side, stepped back in swiftly and slammed a right hook to the 'breed's jaw. Billy the Cougar staggered, shaking his head. His head shook again, but this time because a straight left took him in the mouth. Teeth shattered and split his lips. Blood flowed over his chin, but as Bonner whistled in a roundhouse right, he rammed the top of his greasy head at

94

the tall man's face.

It caught Bonner under the jaw and he floundered, feet scrabbling in the sand. He stumbled, put down a hand to keep from falling, and Billy-Bob rushed in and kicked him in the chest. Rush Bonner spun and crashed to the rock. The 'breed dived for the knife, snatched it and then twisted back, hurling himself bodily at the downed fugitive. He rammed a knee into Bonner's side, dropped on his chest and straddled him, knife raised, eyes glittering with the lust to kill.

Rush pronged two fingers on his right hand and stabbed upwards. Billy-Bob, upper body coming forward with the sweep of the blade, screamed as the fingers drove into his eyes. He jerked back and away, slashing wildly. The blade cut through Bonner's shirt and opened a gash in his flesh.

He bucked, and the blinded 'breed fell to one side but continued to kick and slash with the knife. Bonner caught the hand and twisted, straining to take the blade from the man. The Cougar refused to let go and managed to put a short cut in Bonner's forearm.

In desperation, he twisted Billy's arm, bending the wrist backwards. The 'breed, still unable to see for the blood in his eyes, threw himself forward, teeth bared.

The blade was pointing at his chest, just where the ribs arch. There was a sobbing sound as Billy-Bob Cougar felt the steel driving into his heart, and then his last breath gusted sourly into Bonner's face before he went limp and dropped away, the knife protruding from between his ribs.

Rush Bonner leaned against the rock, sweat and blood dripping from him, fighting for breath, staring at the dead man at his feet.

Well, one thing, Billy had been operating alone and there had been no shooting to bring in the rest of the posse.

But he couldn't stay here now. He needed to get on the trail — and fast.

He decided to look for Billy's horse first: there might be food in the man's saddle-bags, and he was bound to have a canteen.

He glanced again at the dead man.

'It's an ill wind, Billy-boy . . . '

The horse was easy to find, ground-hitched just around a bend of the canyon. It looked like crowbait, coat shaggy and old sticks and leaves caught up in the tail and mane, the scarred flanks telling of its hard use by the 'breed. But there were taut, springy muscles under that neglected-looking hide. Bonner spent a few minutes talking softly to the rolling-eyed, suspicious animal before he was able to grab the bridle.

There was a ball of pemmican in one saddle-bag which didn't smell too appetizing, and seeds of some kind tied in the corner of a ragged bandanna. He rolled the pemmican in the seeds and swallowed a couple of mouthfuls without gagging. It would be enough for now — genuine Indian pemmican was a good source of protein, but he had to admit he had tasted better than this.

In the other bag there was a dirty shirt which he threw away and a handful of change which he kept. There was a claspknife, too, old and worn, and he put it in his pocket. The water canteen he hung from his own saddlehorn after rinsing the shallow cut across his chest, then swilling a mouthful. He unsaddled Billy's mount and turned it loose. It stood and stared at him with flaring nostrils for a long moment before it realized it was free.

Then it kicked up its heels with a snorting neigh and ran off down the canyon. The roan pricked its ears and tugged at the reins but Bonner led it back to where he had fought Billy-Bob Cougar. He pushed the body under an overhanging rock, tried to retrieve the hunting knife from the chest but the cartilage gripped the blade too tightly.

The sun was heeling over into the afternoon sky and he was tempted to stay a little longer, wait for the jack-rabbit to show itself at dusk. But he figured he had pushed his luck enough and that horse of the 'breed's might find the posse again — then all they had to do was backtrack it to here.

He was swinging into the saddle when he heard the distant gunshots — three evenly spaced. *A signal.*

Someone needed help or was calling in the scattered riders of the posse.

Grimly, lifting the reins, he knew damn well it was most likely the latter.

Time he wasn't here.

7

Canyons Galore

'Son of a bitch sure likes the cold steel.'

Horseshoe made the remark as he watched two of the posse men drag Billy-Bob's corpse out from under the rock overhang, the knife erect in his chest.

Folding his big hands on his saddlehorn, Dean Halstead leaned forward. 'Looks like that 'breed met his match in more ways than one.' He gestured to the Cougar's battered face, particularly the smashed mouth. He sighed. 'Goddamm! That Bonner's a whole heap tougher than we figured.'

'Smarter, too,' said Tab Hemming sourly. His group had met up with the others after Horsehoe had fired the three-shot signal. As Dean turned bleak eyes on the freighter, he nodded into the dying light. 'He's still ahead of us and night's comin' on. He'll be halfway to Canada by mornin'.'

'Only if he grows wings!' Halstead snapped. 'You weren't smart enough to find his trail, anyways.'

'Aaaah, Billy-Bob was s'posed to come back an' tell us soon's he found tracks. Y'ask me, he was tryin' for the bounty all by hisself, didn't aim to share it.'

'Sounds like Billy-Bob,' opined Horse-shoe, nodding for emphasis. 'Now we don't have a tracker. What we do, Dean? Bury Billy an' make camp?'

The weary, dusty posse men were all for it and Dean was going to be cantankerous and force them on for a few miles, but the proximity of plenty of cool, clear water made him change his mind.

'Yeah, all right, we'll camp here.' He raked his cold gaze around the smiling men as they started to dismount. 'Hobble your mounts and leave 'em saddled, ready to ride fast as you can spit — an we'll be ridin' *before* sun-up.'

That brought plenty of groans and muttered complaints.

Horseshoe, dismounted now and pressing his hands into the small of his back as he arched his spine carefully, said, 'He won't ride much at night. Think Billy might've managed to cut him up some. There's blood ten yards away where it looks like Bonner's roan was ground-hitched.'

'By sun-up I want the whole posse clear of these canyons — and get someone up on the butte. We'll spot him soon's the sunlight touches the plains.'

Horseshoe nodded: it was a good idea. From up on the butte's high walls they would be able to see Bonner in any direction out on the plains.

With luck, the man would be dead by noon and the posse would be figuring how much was their share of the bounty . . .

But, in the pale light of pre-dawn, there was no sign of Rush Bonner.

Dean Halstead frowned, took out his bad temper on his mount by yanking its head around savagely as he stood in the stirrups and called up to the man he had ordered to climb high on the butte.

'Anythin', Cal?'

'Nary a thing movin', Dean.'

The man was on a ledge just below the highest point, an unclimbable slab of rock towering ten feet behind him.

'Wash your eyes with canteen water and look again!'

'Already tried that. You don't b'lieve there's no one out there, come on up. I'm on my way down.'

'You stay put till it gets lighter!'

'Goddammit, Dean! *There's no one out there*! You fellers've eaten, I've had nothin' but stale hardtack. I'm comin' down.'

Halstead started to berate the man but changed his mind. It was Cal Benniton, and he was young and clear-eyed, a good rifle shot and hunter — looked like he had just better believe the man.

'Where the hell could he be?' asked Horseshoe, some agitated.

'Well, if he ain't out on the damn plains, he has to be still here in the canyons.'

Horsehoe and other posse members within hearing tensed.

'My God!' Tab Hemmings said. 'You don't expect us to hunt a killer like that in here? Hell almighty, Dean, the man's a murderer! Way these canyons and drifts twist and turn he could pick us off one by one!'

'If he ain't out on the plains, *he's still in here*!' Halstead repeated with cold emphasis. 'Our job is to hunt him down and that's what we're gonna do.'

There were plenty of protests and Dean Halstead sat his horse, tight-faced and unbending, letting them bitch all they wanted.

'Feel better?' he snapped, when the complaints became more desultory and began to drift off into unfinished sentences. He raked his frosty gaze around. 'Now, we get on down to that patch of sand, smooth it over, and we draw a rough map of these here canyons — we all know at least a part of this area. We'll pool our knowledge, then break up into groups and *hunt that murdering bastard down*!'

There was one direction Dean Halstead didn't look: none of them even considered it.

It was behind the butte, back the way they had come.

* ★ ★

Rush Bonner had gone to ground after he had heard those signalling shots. His first instinct was to spur the roan away from the butte and its system of canyons, but he knew as soon as he did that, he would be a prime target for the posse.

There was a hell of a lot of open country out there before he would be able to get into some thin timber and low hills. He would be in sight for hours, if not most of the day, and they would sure as hell ride him down.

He had thought of taking Billy-Bob's crowbait mount along but it was Indian trained and would no doubt act-up like a mustang fresh in from the wilds with a stranger, slowing him more than it would be worth.

He had seen a little of the network of canyons and draws and dead ends and knew he wouldn't stand a chance trying to dodge the posse men in here.

What could he do? Learn to fly?

That seemed to be the only other way out.

No! He could go back. They wouldn't expect him to go back the way he had come. And the butte would be between him and the posse, for all their attention was concentrated on the plains to the north. That was the logical escape route and that's where they would search.

Still, he didn't want to go back to town, or anywhere near it.

They all believed he had murdered the sheriff and stolen that bank money out of the safe — *he was forming a theory of what had happened there, too* — and they would want his blood! Dean Halstead would likely turn a blind eye if the posse shot him to death, or strung him up to the nearest tree before he could even spit.

In fact, he would likely be happier that way. The money would never be found and everyone would simply surmise Rush had hidden it somewhere along his getaway trail. It would probably start searches that would go on sporadically for years, until the stolen hoard became just another legend of lost loot and the value would grow with the passing of time — twenty thousand, thirty, fifty or more.

As long as he was dead and wasn't given a chance to deny the theft and murder.

And Dean Halstead, possibly Horseshoe, too, would make sure he had no opportunity to protest his innocence.

But he didn't have to go back to town. All he need do was put the butte between himself and the posse, get well clear, and then swing south, cross the river far to the west of the town and take a north-east trail.

Once he reached the Stillwater, he would be well on the way to Bob Tyson's.

Actually, that was something he had to sort out yet: should he go to Bob now that he had this murder hanging over him? He didn't want to involve Tyson, but this was all unkown country to him and he needed someone who could guide him through it.

He was certain Dean Halstead wouldn't give up this side of the day Hell froze over.

To make it work, the deputy had to be very sure that Rush Bonner was dead.

★　★　★

It wasn't as easy as he had hoped, finding his way back through the canyons.

For one thing the posse was scattered widely and he glimpsed two riders not 400 yards away, cutting across a junction of two snaking draws. There was scattered gunfire, too, echoing and whip-cracking through the canyons.

It brought a crooked smile to his face: literally jumping at shadows, he guessed.

The posse would be mighty nervous with all the shadows in here, now moving as the sun rose higher: seen out of the corner of a tensed man's eye, it could look like a rider. If they had any sense at all each man would be riding with his rifle across his thighs, dangerously cocked, too, in some really nervous cases.

A flicker of movement and that rifle would come up blazing.

Dean Halstead would be having a blue fit which was okay by Bonner: the more the man had to think about, the more mistakes he would make.

Finally, Rush found his way out to where he had first entered the butte area. He saw the posse's trail plainly, paralleling his own where he hadn't properly covered his tracks. He paused, in deep shadow, his own rifle across his thighs now, as he studied the land.

He had to swing left pretty sharply to get away from the trail back to town. But too sharply and someone in the posse might see him, if they happened to be in a position to have a partial view behind the butte.

But there was no choice: he had to do it, and it had to be now, while the sun was still low enough to strike a man's eyes should he look to the east.

He spurred the roan away from the butte, heart hammering faster, mouth dry.

The horse responded well and he swore a little as the hoofs drummed across hard-packed earth. But it was unlikely the muffled sound would reach any of the posse still searching deep within the canyons.

After a time, he began to relax some, turned his head to look at the butte, now blazing redly in the strengthening sunlight. He slowed the roan a little, squinted, but there was no sign of any pursuit.

Encouraged, he took off his hat and slapped it across the roan's flanks, giving a quiet version of the Rebel yell as the horse increased its pace.

He was going to make it to the river!

*   *   *

It was just too bad Dean Halstead grew impatient: he was already mighty riled at all the shooting at shadows.

'Goddamn! If Bonner's in here, he'll go to ground in some goddamn cave and we'll never find him!'

'There've been no tracks, Dean,' Horseshoe pointed out, unhappy about traipsing through these narrow canyons. 'Billy-Bob might've picked up somethin', but we just ain't that good.'

'Well, we don't have Billy-Bob, do we?'

'No-oo — but there's Fuzz back in

111

the cells.' Dean snapped his head up and Horseshoe added, 'He's a better tracker even than the Cougar.'

Dean frowned. 'Yeah, but after last night . . . '

'Hell, he's used to hangovers and nursin' a few bumps and bruises. I reckon he'll be ready to tear the jail apart by now. I could ride back, give him a little whiskey to kinda get him back on track, then bring him out here.'

'He'll kick your butt till your nose bleeds. He won't wanta come.'

'Might — if we offer him a big enough slice of the reward. Sort of . . . special pay for actin' as tracker?'

Halstead thought about it, made a few more arguments but knew he was going to agree to send Horsehoe back for Fuzz Carmody: the mountain man was an uncanny tracker, and they sure didn't seem to be making any progress right here and now.

'OK. But make it quick. We don't want Bonner reachin' anyone he can convince he didn't kill Kit Pollard or

112

steal that money from the safe.'

So Horsehoe quit the butte, making one or two wrong turns before finding his way out, and started to turn towards the trail back to town.

The sun was still just low enough to throw a lot of ground shadows from small hummocks and tufts of grass — and the churned-up ground of tracks that veered away from the town trail.

Startled when he noticed these, Horseshoe hauled rein abruptly, walked his horse across, then dismounted. He took some of the disturbed earth between his fingers and rubbed it.

Freshly done, not even slightly dried or impacted by the strengthening sun.

Heart beating faster now, he mounted, rode back to the edge of the butte and stood on his saddle, reaching up to a jutting rock and pulling himself up to it. Grunting and sweating, he straightened, boots not really feeling secure on the weathered rock, shaded his eyes.

It took him several minutes before he saw a small disturbance way out there against the glare of the distant river.

If that wasn't a rider — and he had no doubt as to the identity of the horseman — he would give his share of the bank loot to Deacon Parnell and his Church of the True Saviour.

Then he grinned as he thought of a joke: out loud, he said,

'Hey, Bonner, what's your rush!'

8

No Badges

Horseshoe hesitated — now what should he do? Ride back to Halstead and the posse, or go after Bonner?

Well, Bonner was a long, long way ahead. Even using his field-glasses, he could only make out the roan for sure. Its rider could be anyone, though he knew instinctively by the set of the man it was Rush Bonner. He decided he had better go find the posse.

Dean Halstead wasn't pleased to see him.

'Jesus Christ! Can't you do nothin' I tell you? What the hell're you doin' back here so soon?'

Horseshoe put on a superior look that made Dean mad, but, at the same time, wary. *Now what could make that knot-head look so confident?*

'I come back 'cause I figured you'd like to know where Bonner is.'

The posse men within hearing drew closer and Halstead frowned. 'Say your piece, damn you, Horseshoe.'

The deputy did and when he had finished Dean Halstead's lips were drawn into a bloodless, razor-thin line. 'The cunning son of a bitch! You're *sure* it was him?'

'Had to be.'

'Not what I asked, dammit! Are you sure it was Bonner?'

'I am, Deane. Used my glasses, picked out his roan no mistake. Figured you'd want to go after him, rather than have me ride all the way back to town for Fuzz.'

Dean was a vindictive man and didn't like the way Horseshoe had given him this news, making him look foolish in front of the others.

'Well, you leave Bonner to us — and go get Fuzz.'

Horseshoe's jaw dropped. 'But . . . we know where he is! We don't need a tracker.'

'We do if I say so. Now get on back to town. Rest of you, check your guns, we're goin' after Bonner an' just hope he's still in sight when we get to the river.'

* * *

Horseshoe was still savagely angry at Halstead even when the low buildings of town came in sight.

'Treatin' me like a schoolkid! Tongue-lashin' me in front of all the others . . .'

He was fuming as he rode his mount down a grade and into the long, straggling line of timber a couple of miles out of town. He was almost through the trees when suddenly three horsemen rode out ahead and blocked the trail.

He hauled rein fast, slapping a hand to the butt of his rifle in the saddle scabbard.

'Leave it,' said a man slightly ahead of the others.

He wasn't very tall in the saddle,

about average, it seemed to Horseshoe, but there was something about that rugged face with the piercing eyes that made him stop his hand in mid-move and rest it on his thigh. He licked at his lips.

'Better. Who you be?'

Horseshoe straightened a little, flipped open his vest so they could see the tin star. 'Deputy from town.' He nodded past the man whose gaze never flickered. Horseshoe glanced at the others. One was big but flabby-looking, though often fat hid iron-taut muscle in men of such build. His face was round, smooth; looked as if it didn't grow much bristle.

The third man was dark-skinned, some kind of 'breed, Horsehoe figured, not all Indian, maybe with a good touch of Mexican. *Mestizo*, he decided.

'Now it's my turn,' he said with more confidence than he felt facing this dangerous-looking trio. 'Who're you?'

'You know a US marshal's badge when you see one?' the hard man in front asked and Horsehoe knew he looked surprised, merely nodded. 'Well, you won't see any such badges here, which don't mean we don't carry 'em, only that we don't flash 'em around. Savvy?'

'No. Damned if I do.'

'Told you he looked dumb when we first spotted him, Flagg,' the fat one said with a slight chuckle. 'Din' I say that, Paco?'

'You say, Candy.'

'Listen, what the hell's goin' on? I'm on my way into town to pick up a prisoner who's a good tracker. Need him for a posse I'm on, tryin' to run down a murderer that busted outa jail.'

'That feller Bonner?' asked Flagg.

'Yeah — how you know that?'

'Told you, we're US marshals. They brung us in on that Miller's Ford bank robbery. We got word a few days ago you had one of the robbers in jail and were sittin' on him, not tellin' anyone about it.'

There was accusation there now that made a feather run down Horsehoe's spine, causing him to shiver. 'Er — well, Kit Pollard was in charge. He was the sheriff, but this Bonner busted outa his cell, stuck a knife in Kit and grabbed the money from the safe.'

'That's what we heard in town.' Flagg shook his head slowly. 'Couldn't believe it'd happened, and when we got more time, you can explain to me how it come about.'

'Hell, I'm only a deputy . . . '

He faltered as those deadly eyes fixed to his greying face.

'You can explain it to me but later,' Flagg told him flatly. 'You on this Bonner's tail?'

'Well, kinda. Look, I dunno as I ought to be tellin' you any of this. Best you ask Dean Halstead; he's in charge of things now.'

Flagg eased his mount forward until it was close in alongside Horseshoe's grey, but facing in the opposite direction. He leaned towards the deputy slightly and Horseshoe swayed away, eyes looking worried.

'But you're here an' you don't seem to savvy, mister. We're takin' over. Bonner, or whatever his name is, is our meat now. You and Halstead are out of it.'

'I-I just dunno what to say. I mean, I'm only s'posed to bring back Fuzz — that's our tracker . . .'

'He any good?'

'Hell, yeah! Mountain man. Best tracker this side of the Rio.'

Flagg spat, looking sceptical. 'Rio's one helluva long way from here, but OK. Bring him along. You go with him, Candy. Fuzz gives you any trouble, shoot him. We ain't got time to — What the hell's wrong with you? Why you lookin' like that?'

Horseshoe was shocked. '*Shoot* him! For Chris'sakes, he's only sleepin' off a moonshine binge! Anyway, you can't just shoot a man like that! You're s'posed to be a lawman.'

Flagg's mouth twitched, maybe a flicker of a smile. 'Yeah, that's what I'm s'posed to be, all right — Candy and

121

Paco, too. You wanna stay outa trouble, you'll do what you're told and let us get on with our job — our way. Now go get this Fuzz. Paco an' me'll take a smoke in the shade.'

* * *

The jailer was a stand-in, a sometime helper when things got mighty lively with a trail herd in town. Dean had put him in charge of the jail while he organized a posse with Horseshoe. The man's name was Hollis, called Holly by 'most everyone, and he looked uncomfortable as Horseshoe came in now with the big, sweaty Candy easing in behind him.

'Wasn't expectin' to see you so soon, Hoss.'

'Need to pick up Fuzz. What's wrong?'

Holly stood, licking his lips, glancing briefly at Candy who was looking around the office. 'Well, he come round earlier than 'xpected,' Holly stammered. 'Kicked up a helluva ruckus.

Thought he was gonna pull the damn door outa the wall.'

'So you turned him loose!'

'Well, hell, Hoss! I'm here by myself! No one in town wants to tangle with Fuzz. Couldn't get in touch with you or Dean so . . . '

Horseshoe sighed, swore briefly. 'Yeah, yeah. It's OK, Holly. Was best thing to do. Where'd he go?'

Holly swallowed, licked his lips. 'Lookin' for you. Said you was the one told him Melody was back at the saloon.'

Horseshoe froze, grinding his teeth briefly. 'What I said was, '*If* she ever came back, she'd go straight to the saloon an' her old job' . . . Ah. You stay here an' look after things. I gotta get back to the posse.

On the landing outside, he said to Candy, 'I better check that Fuzz ain't tearin' up the saloon again before I go. You wanna come with me? You might risk a busted jaw or a cripplin', but I'd appreciate the back-up.'

It was reverse psychology, only Horsehoe didn't even know the term: he figured asking Candy that way, spelling out the risks, the fat man would run a mile rather than go up against Fuzz.

Candy didn't run anywhere but he emphatically refused to accompany the deputy. 'I don't give a good goddamn what you do. I'm goin' buy me some strap candy then go back to Flagg.'

Horseshoe managed to look disappointed and watched the fat man waddle to the hitch rail, mount up and ride down the street to the general store without looking back.

Horsehoe hurried down the street, but not to the saloon.

He turned into the side street that led to the telegraph office.

* * *

It was near sundown by the time Horseshoe rode into the posse's camp, surprised to see it not far ahead of where he had left it this morning.

'What's goin' on, Dean?' he said as he dismounted and accepted a cup of coffee from one of the posse men. 'Thought you'd be at the river by now.'

Halstead looked up from where he sat on a dead-fall, face bleak, 'You run into Flagg an' his pards on your way to town?'

'Yeah. Tough customers.'

'More'n that, they're US marshals and they've taken over this manhunt.'

Horseshoe drained his coffee and called to the man at the camp-fire who had drawn the short straw for cooking tonight, 'Gimme whatever's goin', Gillespie, an' pile it on.'

'Help yourself — I ain't your damn servant.'

Horseshoe hitched his belt and scowled as he moved forward, roughly shouldering Gillespie aside.

'I'll remember this next time I see you staggerin' around town with a few redeyes under your belt.'

'Aw, now, Hoss, I din' mean — '

'You meant — and I got a long memory. Pull that skillet closer . . .'

Sitting beside Halstead, forking greasy food into his mouth, Horseshoe chewed and swallowed.

'They ain't marshals.'

Dean was about to light his freshly rolled cigarette and he paused with his thumbnail against the vesta head. 'What'd you say? For Chris'sakes, empty your mouth first. I can't understand you, chewin' an' spittin' like a hog.'

Horseshoe spoke slowly and deliberately.

'They . . . ain't . . . US marshals.'

'Who? Flagg and that fat *hombre* and the greaser?'

Horseshoe nodded. 'You ever heard of a greaser bein' in the marshals' service?'

'Well . . . yeah. They use 'em for guides an' interpreters down along the Rio. Well, goddamnit! Quit lookin' like the cat that's swallowed the canary! Tell me what you know!'

'Was suspicious of 'em right off. They

made some excuse about not showin' badges 'cause they was undercover but — Anyway, Flagg told the fat one to shoot Fuzz if he gave any trouble an' that didn't seem right.'

'No-oo, but he might've just meant, like, shoot him in the leg or somethin'. He know Fuzz is a walkin' tree?'

Horseshoe nodded. 'I dunno what he meant but when I got rid of Candy in town I sent some wires to the sheriff in Miller's Ford and asked if the bank had brought in marshals. He sounded riled even at the suggestion: *No! He's in charge.* So I wired back the three names — Flagg, Candy, Paco.'

Dean Halstead was stiff now, unlit cigarette hanging limp and forgotten on his lower lip. 'They ain't marshals?'

'They ain't lawmen of any kind. They're three of the gang they suspect raided the bank!'

'Jee-*suss*!'

'The one Bonner killed must've been the fourth man, Secombe, an' he was carryin' the money.'

Dean scrubbed a hand around his jaw. 'We gotta get movin'! They catch up with Bonner and he convinces 'em he didn't kill Pollard and steal the money from the safe, you an' me're in a lotta trouble, Horseshoe.'

'I know that! Been thinkin' on it all the way back from town. Hell, I knew it was goin' too good! Too damn smooth!'

Dean finally fired up his cigarette, took a very long first inhale and blew the smoke out his nostrils.

'Quit whinin'. We'll get underway before the men are settled in anymore.'

Horseshoe went rigid. 'You're loco! Forget Bonner and Flagg. Let's you an' me hightail it pronto! We can go a long way splittin' that bank money down the middle.'

'How far you reckon? With Flagg and his sidekicks comin' after us?'

'Aw, we can be a far piece from here by the time he figures it was us organized Bonner's break out and fitted him up with the murder and stealin' the money. We *gotta* go, Dean! You don't wanna, lemme have my share and — '

Dean raised his voice. 'Sorry, gents. Hoss has just brought us some bad news. Them so-called marshals are the ones robbed the bank at Miller's Ford. We gotta get after 'em. They catch up with Bonner and we'll never see that money again and there'll be no reward paid.'

There was much heated discussion and complaining from the posse men and Horseshoe swore something awful as he glared at Halstead.

'Thanks a lot, Deane. Damn you!'

Halstead surprised him by smiling crookedly.

'You're welcome, Hoss.' He lowered his voice. 'Listen, men like Flagg and his sidekicks wouldn't never give up till they caught up with us. We'd be lookin' over our shoulders for the rest of our lives. This way — with the posse to back us — we can wipe 'em out, Bonner along with 'em, with a little luck. The posse can share the reward while we retire and head for Canada. And we'll know damn well Flagg ain't gonna appear on our doorstep some bright mornin'.'

Horseshoe's mind was in a whirl, but gradually he saw the sense in Dean Halstead's argument, and by that time, the posse men were saddling up, getting ready for a night ride — still bitching.

But looking forward to the possibility of getting their hands on some reward money.

And right now they didn't care who they had to kill to get it.

9

Guns in the Dark

Approaching darkness didn't stop Flagg and his pards.

They had reached the river before sundown. Paco dismounted, one hand holding his mount's reins, dragging the grulla along. He literally crawled on hands and knees, face almost in the dirt, as he looked for the right angle in the fading light.

He found where Bonner had entered the river and the man had made a token effort to throw off pursuers by riding upstream, against a fairly strong current, too, before exiting the water.

Then the tracks faded after a few yards and Paco sat back on his hams, tugging at his raven-black moustache.

'You better not be just restin',' growled Flagg.

Candy, jaws working on the rasp-berry sugar strap, chuckled. 'Thought he was gonna drop his pants for a minute.'

Flagg glared, not feeling humorous. 'Shut up! Paco?'

'There two ways he can go.' He pointed left towards thickening trees, then swivelled his short upper body and jerked his head towards a patch of brush.

'He could hide his tracks better in the trees . . . ' Flagg lifted his reins impatiently, paused as the mestizo added, 'I think this one not mind doing things the hard way.'

Flagg frowned. 'The brush country? We could see him in there, miles off.'

'He will have cross by now, be in the foothills.'

Flagg's yellow teeth tugged at his heavy under-lip. 'Mebbe. I still like the trees.'

Paco shrugged. 'You look with Candy; I check the brush. We meet . . . ' — he stood on tiptoe to see better, pointing to

132

the shadowed face of the nearest foot-hill — 'under that beeg rock. The one that pokes out — '

'Yeah, I see it. All right. We meet there by sundown, whether we've picked up Bonner's trail or not.'

Flagg was already riding into the trees and Candy stuffed the remainder of his sugar straps into a saddle-bag, wiped the back of a wrist across his sticky mouth and followed.

Paco led his horse towards the edge of the brush, one hand lightly fingering the butt of his sixgun. It was a Smith & Wesson .38 break-action revolver, worn high on his left side, tilted forward for a cross-draw.

He was very, very fast with it and looked forward to meeting this man called Bonner. He was confident he would find him before the others.

Sundown came and Flagg was first at the rendezvous. Candy came ambling in only minutes later, licking at another of his rasperry sugar straps. Flagg grunted by way of greeting.

'S'pose you found nothin', too?' Candy shook his head and Flagg snapped. 'Answer me, you tub of lard! Get that damn sticky mess outta your mouth before I ram it down your throat!'

Candy was used to Flagg's bleak moods, but hastily wrapped the candy in a grubby cloth and shoved it into his shirt pocket. He swallowed a large piece and had to cough several times before he could answer, licking his fingers one after the other, as he did so.

'Nary a sign, Flagg. Think mebbe Paco was right and Bonner took to the brush.'

'Well, where the hell is Paco! I said to come here whether we'd tracked Bonner or not. Night's closin' in fast now.'

Candy shrugged. 'You know Paco. He picks up a trail, he don't want to stop till he gets to the end of it. He might've found Bonner already.'

Flagg was about to snap some sarcastic reply when there came the drift echoes of distant, ragged gunfire. *Two guns — one a heavier calibre than the other. Like a .45 against, say, a .38.*

Grim-faced, Flagg lifted the reins, unsheathing his rifle.

'You could be right!'

★   ★   ★

Candy was right.

Paco had found Rush Bonner.

The fugitive had been resting. The roan had strained a leg in the river, fighting the strong current: one shoe, badly worn, with little grip, had slipped on an underwater stone and the leg had twisted. The roan was never one to overreact to pain but it floundered in chest-deep water and its muzzle went under just as it drew a breath.

The head swung up wildly and Bonner just managed to get out of the way, or he would have had a smashed nose, or worse. As it was, he lost his balance and tumbled from the saddle, one wrist caught in the reins which he had wrapped around his forearm. The roan lunged away, dragging Bonner with him. Afraid of more stones underfoot, it plunged parallel to the bank in deeper water. Bonner went under five times, gasping and spluttering, before the roan stumbled out, dragging him up on to a bar of coarse sand.

The reins untwined then and Bonner's strained left arm flopped to his side. The roan limped and licked at its fetlock as Bonner lay there, fighting for breath. It was only minutes before the horse settled, keeping its weight off the sore leg and Bonner could breathe more normally.

He glanced up at the sun — dipping quite fast down the slope of the western sky now. He needed to get well away from the river while there was still light.

Examining the roan's leg he concluded it was not a bad sprain but would slow down their progress considerably. All the more reason to get on the move right now.

He walked with the horse for some way, ground-hitching it while he went back with a broken, leafy bough and brushed away as many tracks as he could. But he could never cover the broken edge of the bank where the hurt roan had floundered its way out of the river.

But he had learned long ago a man did the best he could in any situation — no gain in fussing over what he wanted to do and couldn't.

Foothills were close, the slopes darkening on this side as the sun sank slowly behind them. Good — he wouldn't be silhouetted. He decided to get as high as possible in safety on the dark side, cold camp, and be on his way again before sunrise, up and over.

He searched for a fairly level piece of ground, even though it was on the slopes, so the horse would have some ease for its leg. He tore up his shirt — having earlier put on the one that had been in the saddle-bags — soaked the old cloth in water, knotted it firmly around the joint between the cannon bone and the great pastern, covering the normal tuft of hair on the fetlock.

It should give some support and the coolness would alleviate any residual pain.

He just hoped he wouldn't have to leap madly into the saddle at some night alarm and ride like the wind out of here. *Or try — the roan wouldn't be capable of rapid flight.*

Climbing up this high, he had looked behind constantly and once thought he saw the tree branches moving in the opposite direction to the wind. But although he had paused, there was no sign of a rider. *Maybe some wild animal, possibly a deer.*

He hobbled the horse loosely and picked a place in the heavy brush some distance away, nursing his Colt, rifle on the ground within reach. Back pressed against a slim tree, he dozed: he needed rest like the roan and —

It seemed like only minutes, but had to be longer because it was quite dark now, when he heard the alien sounds a little downslope from where he sat.

He stood slowly, aware he might be dimly silhouetted against the greyness of the brush, but he had to see. The roan was standing with ears erect, looking off in the same direction. The noise came again, like someone pushing through the brush, or something heavy landing in it and rolling after being thrown to divert his attention!

Bonner dropped at the thought and a moment later a gun crashed over to his left, almost on the same level as himself. The flash outlined part of a man's body and then he was sprawling, thrusting the Colt out ahead of him, triggering two fast shots. He rolled instantly and the other gun answered. He heard the slug bite into the brush and then *thunk!* into the ground. *Close!*

Bonner twisted and fired twice at where he had seen the gunflashes. A man grunted, dry brush crackled as a body moved violently, and then the intruder staggered out, fighting to lift his pistol. Bonner fired and the man was hurled back by the bullet, sprawled awkwardly, half-crushing a bush, then rolled off to flop on his back, a bare six feet away.

He must be damned good to have worked his way in that close!

On one knee now, Bonner used his eyes, forcing himself to move his gaze carefully, looking for sign that might mean the man had back-up close by. He reloaded by feel as he did this and when he had filled all six chambers, closed the loading gate and stood carefully, hammer spur under his thumb.

It seemed like the intruder was alone. He knelt beside him, straining to see. The man could be an Indian or maybe a Mexican, going by his size and the conchos on his belt and the empty holster that had been set for a cross-draw. Whoever he was, he was dying.

'You're a long ways from home, *amigo.*'

Bonner moved fast, unhobbling the nervous roan, hoping the animal would be able to carry him safely out of here. He knew the intruder must have back-up somewhere close by — most likely he was the tracker, moving on ahead of the others — and he had made his try at collecting the bounty for himself.

Tough luck, feller.

The man groaned, coughed, gasped. '*Amigo! Por . . . favor . . .* '

Sixgun in hand, Bonner went down on one knee beside the Mexican. There was blood, dark and glistening, trickling from his mouth. One hand lifted weakly, flopped back.

'I . . . die. I have wife . . . in Juarez. Ro-Rosa Alcazar.' He was gasping by now, glazing eyes imploring. 'In my . . . *cinturon* — ' He touched his wide, concho-studded belt with bloody fingers. 'You cut stitching. Some . . . *pesos*. You be good enough to — to . . . '

Bonner nodded. 'I'll see she gets 'em, friend. If your pards don't kill me. Who the hell are you anyway?'

He was surprised to see the purple lips part and large, gapped teeth smeared with bood, appear. *A smile!* 'We steal the bank money: Flagg, Candy, Secomb — you kill him — an' me. We survive . . . '

'Well, I don't have your damn money! Someone else took it from the law office safe but I got blamed.'

He was suddenly aware that Paco was coughing, deep and bubbling — and he dodged a sudden spray of blood. The dark-skinned bony hand grabbed at his sleeve, slid off, the eyes stared, pleading and Bonner said quickly, 'You've got my word, *amigo*!'

Paco sagged back, sighing, dead before Bonner got to his feet. He stooped again, took off the man's hand-made belt and stuffed it in a saddle-bag.

'Have to leave you lie, friend. *Adios*.'

A hundred feet away from the site of the shootout, he mounted the still limping roan: it withstood his weight without complaint. Relieved, he lifted the reins and started across the face of the slope, but angled up slightly, not wanting to put too much strain on that damaged leg.

Then he heard the yell below and an instant later a rifle ripped open the night, bullets whistling around him.

It must be the damned brush! It was grey or dusty green, and in this light formed a pale background — which he was moving across — making him a dim but visible target.

But there was no choice. Whichever way he went, up, down, across, he had a lot of brush to get through, ranging from man-high to stunted. The horse would make the best target — the roan colour showing solid and dark.

Even as he thought this a bullet went so close it passed under his hand holding the rein and clipped a dozen strands from the flapping mane. The horse whinnied, ducked its head. The sudden movement made Bonner lurch forward — and it saved his life. He heard the crack of the bullet passing through the space his body had occupied a split second earlier.

He didn't straighten, instead, lay low, face pressed into the side of the roan's straining neck, patting it swiftly, speaking quietly, then yanked the reins violently and unexpectedly, swinging the horse downslope.

It stumbled and snorted a protest as weight was transferred to the injured leg. It half-floundered, but righted, and by then Bonner had his rifle free of the scabbard. He fired it one-handed just as a diversionary shot, before raising it to his shoulder, raking the brush down there where he had seen a powderflash. He emptied the magazine, moving the muzzle slightly after each rapid shot, up a fraction, down a little, right, left, down again, before the hammer clicked on an empty breech. Ejected brass was still falling when he reined the roan across the face of the slope, yelling as he did so.

'C'mon, Tex! Ben! Randy! Gimme covering fire!'

To Flagg and Candy, already cowering from the hail of lead, it seemed as if Bonner had somehow fetched up with other men, and, Candy leading, they plunged downslope, crashing wildly through the brush, already shaken by having found Paco's corpse only yards away.

Bonner pulled the roan slightly upslope and leapt off, yanking on the reins, literally dragging it behind him. It relieved the weight on the loyal horse and, even though it limped, it followed its master willingly enough.

Bonner figured he had only a few minutes to get as high as he could above the posse or whoever it was below.

With any luck he would be over the crest, just after they had come to their senses or, with luck, a little before.

Either way, he had an advantage he had to push: hard.

10

Stillwater

Rush Bonner stopped ten yards down the slope over the crest. The roan was protesting and jerking the reins heavily by that time and limping badly. He figured he had put strain enough on that leg.

There were rocks, not high, but one stood tall enough to give the horse some protection. He ground-hitched the roan there, patting its sweating muzzle, took his rifle and a crushed cardboard carton of ammunition and stretched out behind a low ridge of crumbling rock running across the slope. It was badly weathered, ancient as the copper-coloured primitive men who had once lived and hunted across this land.

Conveniently, there was a piece about

half the size of his head that he managed to work out from some lichen-scabbed cracks and set aside. It left a fine embrasure and he settled the rifle, opened the carton and waited.

They were no fools whoever they were, took their time coming over the crest — then one came to the right of where he had crossed, while the other appeared a minute later off to the left. Both movements were only brief disruptions to the background of stars, the men on foot, crouching, playing it safe by making targets as small as possible.

He waited, knowing they were lying low now they had crossed, hoping he would make the first move. No more men came and Bonner frowned. Of course, they wouldn't be part of the posse. Just two men with their own agenda: to kill him.

Most likely Candy was the biggest one — a lard barrel with legs, having briefly glimpsed the fat man.

Halstead would probably break-up

the posse into small groups in this kind of country. Dean would scatter the twenty-man posse all across the plains, working in converging lines to the range beyond the river, hoping to corner him.

Fat chance! In any case, there was still plenty of danger: he was sure he had been spotted crossing the river, and those three shots would have called them in closer, tightening the noose they were slowly drawing around him. *Time to get outa here, fella!*

Maybe he moved without thinking while he was going over this in his mind: something drew fire, anyway. A bullet shattered the ancient rock to his left and instinctively he rolled right — and someone was waiting for him to make just that exact move.

He didn't hear the second shot, only felt the scaring pain of hot lead coursing across his left shoulderblade. If he hadn't been lying prone, it would have slammed into him from the front and put him down, maybe fatally. He flinched and thrust back from the embrasure, rolling over. The bleeding wound ground into gravel, ripped a painful curse from him. But he saw the silhouette of the too-eager marksman rising against the stars as he tried for the killing shot.

Bonner fired first, the rifle coming confidently to his right shoulder, his eyes used to the darkness by now, aiming directly over the muzzle, finger squeezing the trigger, not jerking, in a disciplined motion he had learned over some mighty hard years.

The big man up there yelled and there was a brief flurry of movement against the stars, the crash of a heavy body.

'Candy?' a voice called from the right, immediately followed by the sounds of its owner moving swiftly to a new position. *Smart!*

Bonner smiled thinly: he was up against some pros here, all right.

'He — he got me, Flagg!'

'Bad?'

'Bad from . . . where I'm sittin'!'

'Then it ain't your big fat ass was hit! Now shut up!' Flagg was the hardnose, Bonner figured, Candy the softer one, but still a good shot. He could hear a whimper or two and thought the man was far from being fatally wounded.

Then there was a commotion and a whinnying: their horses must have broken free from being ground-hitched, and now charged over the crest, far to the right.

'God-*damn*! I told you to use heavy rocks on the reins!'

That was Flagg and he sounded riled enough to kill his pard. But Bonner slithered down to the high rock that protected his roan, saw the running horses as vague shapes angling across the slope. He lifted the rifle, the muzzle flashes shielded from the men on the crest, and put a volley of shots around the pounding feet of the riderless horses.

The animals whickered and snorted and tossed their heads, changing direction, but always taking the easy way — down — down — into the slab of darkness, well away from their riders, now stranded high up on the crest.

Flagg yelled obscenities as he emptied his rifle frustratedly at the embrasure where he thought Bonner was still sprawled. His gun was empty and Candy seemed to be out of it for the moment — a good time to make a move.

Bonner swung into the saddle and the roan was eager to get going. He angled down and had reached the bottom in the heavy layer of darkness before the rifle on the ridge opened up again, shooting blindly.

'Goddamn you, Bonner! I'll follow you to hell if I have to!'

I'll be waiting, Flagg — I'll be waiting.

★   ★   ★

Dean Halstead was playing it safe.

He refused to allow any of the posse to climb the mountain in the dark. There had been too much gunfire and it was uncertain who had the high ground.

151

'Likely gone, long since,' Horseshoe said and Tab Hemming instantly agreed.

' 'Course they would've! You don't hear any shootin' now, do you? We could be up there and have a fine view of the other side come sun-up, Dean, spot anythin' that moves.'

'We stay put,' Dean said flatly. 'I'll send one man to scout around and that's all. Horseshoe?'

'Aw, to hell with that! I been ridin' all over the goddamned countryside like an errand boy. Pick someone else.'

Dean felt himself bristle, but he held back: no sense in alienating Horseshoe. They needed each other to pull this off — and the man was right: he had been doing a lot more riding than the others.

'How about you, Tab? You got plenty to say: time to put your money where your mouth is.'

Hemming wasn't eager but he didn't want Halstead belittling him in front of these townsmen he would have to live with again after this damn manhunt was over.

'All right,' he said ungracefully. 'I'll go take a look. You hear any shootin', come fast! And I mean *pronto*! I didn't hire on to get myself killed!'

He rode out soon after and the rest of the posse settled in for the night. Halstead posted guards, making himself unpopular again, but insisting, adding, 'That greaser's already dead and he was s'posed to be a gunslinger. We're up against men who don't care who they kill.'

A little more in that vein and he had two volunteers.

Long before breakfast, one of the guards, Jackie Larsen, a barber's assistant, wakened Dean and said he thought he'd heard a gunshot earlier. 'It come from a long ways off, Dean,' he told the posse leader who was mighty annoyed at being woken up. 'Either that or it was from the far side of the mountain.'

'Did Rafe hear it?' Halstead asked, voice edgy.

'Said he didn't, but I'm sure it was a

153

shot, Dean. You want to send someone to take a look? Tab Hemming ain't come back yet, either.'

That brought Dean fully awake. 'What? Hell, what's the time . . . ?' He glanced up at the stars and reckoned it was maybe two hours to sun-up, perhaps a little earlier. Which meant that the freighter had been gone for hours.

'The hell didn't you wake me before this?'

Jackie shrugged. 'Well, you know . . . you been grouchy. Figured you needed your rest.'

Dean scowled but made himself calm down. It would be pointless to go stumbling around in the pitch darkness, and if that *was* a gunshot the barber had heard . . .

'All right. Get someone to relieve you. Rafe, too. We'll leave it till daylight. Be safer for everyone.'

But not for Tab Hemming.

They found him with a bullet through the head halfway down the far slope. His horse was gone and further down, they found the carcass of a black gelding with an old mountain lion scar on its chest. A foreleg was snapped, bone showing through. Someone had cut its throat to end its misery.

'That fat ranny who liked the candy was forkin' this when him and Flagg and the Mex rode into our camp,' allowed Horseshoe. 'Looks like his hoss busted its leg on the slope — you can see the skid marks where it's come down way too fast. He must've spotted Hemming, shot him and took his mount, which means he's forkin' a smoke now.'

'With white spots on its neck,' a townsman said helpfully: he worked for the same freight company as Hemming had.

Tilt Burns had ridden on ahead, came back now, looking excited. 'Tracks where two met up. By the size of the hoofprints, I'd say one was Flagg's big chestnut.'

'Two killers together,' Horseshoe

allowed quietly. 'Wonder if they nailed Bonner? There was a heap of shootin' last night.'

Posse members had been scouting the slopes and a man rode in and said there was a good deal of blood up on the crest amongst some rocks. 'Someone got hit.'

'Might be the fat one,' Horseshoe allowed. 'There's blood on the saddle on that black gelding.'

'One wounded, one apparently still in good shape, and both killers — and still no sign of Bonner.'

'Tracks of his roan on the slope. He got down safe, an' his tracks lead off to the north-west. Hoss is lame.'

Horseshoe and Halstead exchanged a quick look. 'Stillwater!'

★ ★ ★

They would soon overtake him, Bonner thought, as he worked the limping roan through the last of the foothills.

He dismounted where he could,

leading the horse, giving it a break from carrying his weight. It slowed him still more but he didn't aim to cripple the roan, then find himself stranded and wait for Flagg and Candy to come and finish him off. He looked around him but there was no really secure place where he could hole-up and shoot it out with the pursuers.

And the posse wouldn't be too far behind. Even if he stopped Flagg and Candy in his tracks — *just how badly was Candy wounded, anyway?* — the shooting would bring in Halstead and his men. Yet another rock and a hard place! He sighed bitterly. He ought to be used to it by now.

Then, moving over a rise, the roan walking a little more easily now, he glimpsed something between a gap in the dwindling hogbacks.

Cattle — and more interesting, barbed wire fences to keep them in!

'By God, there's a ranch out there!'

It was still a toss-up. Would a ranch this far from town know already he was a fugitive with a large posse closing in fast? *More than likely!* Most spreads had chores that would take their riders to town and they would be sure to pick up the latest news or gossip: one would be as interesting as the other to people who spent most of their lives out on the range.

But he had to find another horse, much as he disliked the idea of leaving the roan behind.

Grazing cattle — fences — and men. That was the logical combination, he thought, as he hurried the roan down between the last hogbacks, seeing more and more of the open range as he did so.

Must be nigh on a hundred cows browsing over the grassy slopes beyond the wire fence, a rider way, way off in the distance. Looked like he was dragging a fresh-cut log behind at the end of a rope. Moving his gaze, he glimpsed a partly built cabin up amongst some trees.

It looked small — too small for the

owner of so many cows. *Lineshack!* That's what it was. An outlying building of the main ranch. Mounting now, he looked behind but there was no sign of pursuit as yet. Standing in the stirrups, hearing the deep-chest grunt of annoyance from the roan, he saw there were two men at the shack, apparently waiting for the ranny dragging in the log to add to those of the partly built wall just beyond them.

And there was another man — working on a panel of fencing, twisting a short stake jammed between two wires, pulling the strands taut around the post.

The man saw him and paused, shading his eyes. Bonner took a chance, waved in friendly fashion, set the roan walking towards the fencer. He noticed the ranch-hand's body stiffen a little as he saw the roan's limp.

'Get off an' walk!' the man called and there was anger in his voice. 'That's no way to treat a good mount!'

'Been walking — for hours,' Bonner answered, as he came closer. He started to swing down but the cowboy had picked up a rifle from the ground by now and casually swung it in Bonner's direction.

'Well, walk some more. Say! I know you! You're the ranny we picked up with a head wound when we was drivin' the herd. Remember me? Flapjack? I was wranglin' and ridin' drag for Marty Rice on that drive.'

Bonner didn't really recall the man: that period was one foggy blank in his memory, but he didn't aim to admit to it. 'Sure, I recollect you now. Yeah. Flapjack? Where the hell am I?'

'You be out in the Stillwater country. This is Marty Rice's place, M Slash R.'

For some reason, Rush Bonner felt a surge of relief — but why? It didn't make sense: Marty had showed him kindness, but only what any man could expect out in this country. No, be honest: there was about one person in ten who would do what Marty had done, go out of their way to take him into town, see him doctored and so on.

160

The so-called Code of the Range was more myth than reality these days. Blame the damn war for that!

He could hardly expect her to give him more help, anyway.

But what choice did he have?

Then he tensed: Flapjack was still holding the rifle on him, but his thumb was on the hammer spur now and there was no longer an easy smile on his young, dusty face.

'I heard somethin' about you — busted outa jail. And there was talk you killed Kit Pollard!'

'Flapjack, that's all it is: talk. I busted out, yeah, and if Kit Pollard's dead, it wasn't my doing. He was alive when I left.'

'Well, you'd say that, wouldn't you?'

'Guess so, but it's true. I need to swap the roan for a good horse. Can you fix it for me?'

Flapjack frowned. 'Listen, I don't have — I dunno what I should do — why don't I take you to Marty an' let her decide?'

'I'd rather not involve her. I'm obligated enough and — well, I'm trouble for anyone who helps me.'

'Great! But you're askin' me to — ' Flapjack almost fell as Bonner suddenly kicked the rifle from his grip. When he straightened, he was looking into the barrel of Bonner's Colt.

'Aw, hell!'

'Relax, I'm not gonna hurt you. Where's your horse?'

The cowboy, leery, hands half-raised, licked his lips, jerked his head over towards the distant line-shack. 'We been camped-out there.'

The men working on the lineshack had apparently noticed that Bonner was holding a gun on Flapjack — and while the young cowboy held his attention, they had mounted and ridden quietly down through the timber, coming up behind.

'Leather that gun, feller!' a voice snapped and Bonner heard three rifle hammers snap back to full cock.

Whoever had spoken was a fool: he

should have made him drop the Colt, but Rush didn't aim to argue, put the revolver back into its holster, turning slowly.

'Gents, I'm not here to shoot anyone. But I've got a bunch of killers on my trail and a couple of 'em'll be here any minute. I need a good horse. Will one of you oblige me?'

The cowboys exchanged unbelieving glances and smiled crookedly.

'Why, sure, mister!' said the man he had seen dragging in the new log, lean and tough. 'One of the things I like to do is turn my brown geldin' over to a complete stranger — just 'cause he asks me!'

The others laughed and Bonner smiled, adding, 'Please?'

They guffawed and next minute two of them were rolling about the ground, startled, the horses were backing into each other and the third one, the lean ranny, was fighting to stay on the brown. Bonner's Colt cracked against his skull, knocking off his hat, the man following it to the ground.

He reined in the whickering roan, patting it with one hand, apologizing for having used it so roughly by suddenly driving home his spurs to make it lunge into the others that way. He covered the startled Flapjack who stood, blinking, surprised by the speed of things that had changed everything so abruptly. He lifted his hands quickly as Bonner dismounted and grabbed the brown horse, swinging lithely into the saddle.

'Flapjack, tell these boys I'm sorry. But I can't stick around. I'll leave the horse somewhere they'll find it — and you treat that roan right, or I'll be back for you.'

He spurred the frisky gelding away as the men got dazedly to their feet and, as he rode into the trees, glimpsed a slight movement back on one of the hogbacks he had crossed earlier.

Flagg and Candy: coming on relentlessly.

11

Too Far From Home

The men were dropping out, one by one, sometimes two or three at a time.

By now, Dean Halstead had only half the posse he had started out with. Horseshoe wondered how long it would stay even at that strength.

Not long, as it happened. They were weaving between foothills, making for distant open country glimpsed beyond the hogbacks, when Dean, who had been rolling a cigarette, shook out his match and half-turned to flick the used vesta away. He stiffened.

'Where the hell you think you're goin'?' he bawled at three riders quietly veering away into the brush.

His words made the men halt and turn guiltily as Horseshoe cursed and rode back to join Halstead.

'Hell almighty, Dean! There's just gonna be you an' me, this keeps up!'

Halstead suddenly drew his Colt in a blur of speed and put a shot over the heads of the deserters, but close enough to make them duck involuntarily.

'Judas, Dean! Bonner might hear that! Or Flagg!'

'We ain't *that* close! Not with these old daisies!' Halstead snapped without looking at Horseshoe. He was mad enough not to care about his reckless shooting. His eyes narrowed as he edged his mount closer to the now nervous trio. 'I asked what the hell you think you're doin'!'

The redhead with the jowly face seemed to have been chosen as spokeman.

'We're gettin' too far from home, Dean, an' Tab Hemming's already been killed.'

'Yeah,' agreed one of the others, a pot-bellied man with a wheezy voice. 'I aim to die in bed when it's my time to go — not out here, twenty-five miles north of hell, with my goddamn boots on.'

The third man, older, smaller, just nodded, not looking at Halstead.

'You signed on. You swore the oath. You stay till I say different!'

'Cougar crap!' snapped back the redhead. 'I like to see you try an' make me stay!'

'How about I put a bullet through your leg? Reckon you'd stay then?' Dean spat. 'You'd have no damn choice!'

'And we'd be short a man, just as if he'd rid out on us, Dean,' Horseshoe pointed out quietly to the hotheaded deputy.

The redhead grinned tightly, though he had paled some. 'Always figured Horseshoe was a mite lame-brained, but he's got more sense than you — '

'But he ain't got a cocked gun in his hand!'

The redhead was grey-looking now and the other two moved away slightly. Dean grinned tightly and Horseshoe realized he was only trying to scare the trio. Dean had enough sense to see he had shot his mouth off too quickly — a failing of his.

When he was satisfied Red and his pards were sitting with churning bellies and sweat streaming from their armpits, he suddenly holstered his gun.

'Go on then! Get the hell out of it! You'd be no damn use even if you stayed. But you sure won't get no share of the bounty, neither!'

That part didn't seem to bother them: they were all family men and, though they mightn't admit it out loud, Flagg and Candy and that Mexican had scared them. By now, the Mexican was dead and Candy was wounded, but one of their own, Tab Hemming, was dead, too. That was much closer to home.

In any case, Flagg was the meanest.

The three lifted their reins and rode swiftly into the brush. Dean watched with narrowed eyes and, swearing, rounded to glare at his remaining posse men. He worked hard to straighten out his face as he forced an easy smile.

'Well, all the more for you boys, eh? You don't have to share with that bunch.' He jerked his head to the brush through which Red and his pards were lashing their mounts swiftly.

Halstead's words didn't seem to do anything to make the posse look any more enthusiastic.

They were just starting to ride on again when a distant rattle of gunfire reached them from beyond the foothills.

'That could be someone celebratin' the Fourth of July,' opined Horseshoe. 'Except, they're a month late.'

'Get ridin'!' yelled Dean Halstead, setting the example by raking his weary mount with his spurs and unsheathing his rifle.

He was a full twenty yards ahead before the depleted posse and Horseshoe followed.

★　★　★

Rush Bonner rode right into the trap with his eyes wide open, so he had no one to blame but himself.

When leaving Flapjack and the others at the line-shack, he had glimpsed what he figured were two riders topping out on the ridge way behind him — crossing swiftly, heading for the nearest cover. He had swung away and lifted the brown to a gallop, making for high country, such as it was: a child could spit over what they called a hill out here. Be kind of interesting to see what some of these Big Sky settlers would think of the Sierra Madres or the escarpment south of the Llano Estacado . . .

The thoughts ran through his mind as he concentrated on reaching the top of the rise. He glanced back — there was no sign of the manhunters. Well, it was quite a tangle of draws and dead-ends out here, so with any luck they might have gotten themselves lost.

He topped the crest, paused in the shadow of a large boulder and carefully checked the country ahead and to both sides, then behind. *All clear*. Playing it safe, he looked for some indication of dust back there, but he had swung around on his ride and the sun's glare made it hard to see anything much.

It was a long way back: they couldn't get ahead of him so he touched the spurs to the blowing mount and started over and down the far slope.

It was then he realized that what he had thought was another boulder-shot slope was really one angled, crumbling wall of a low plateau. When he reached the top he swore.

There was the tangle of draws and gulches, not very large, but twisting and turning — but, worse, the whole shebang seemed to run off to his left, back in the direction where Flagg and the wounded Candy had disappeared.

Too late now to turn back over the rise; he would be riding through wide-open country again, without any protection near enough, by the time Flagg reached here.

Maybe it was only by a fluke they had

found the gnarled, crumbling draws and gulches, but how they got there mattered not the proverbial hill of beans. They were *there* and once they realized he was also in the area . . .

He spurred the mount into a gulch for no good reason except it was closest, unsheathing his rifle as he rode. It was a bad choice: he ended up staring at an unclimbable rock wall — a perfect, imprisoning deadend.

The instant he realized his mistake, Bonner wheeled the mount and spurred back the way he had come —

And rode into the ambush Flagg and Candy had rigged. *They must have been close enough to hear the clatter of the brown gelding's hoofs on the rocky ground as he made his way in here.*

Their guns blasted and he heard bullets whipping overhead and around him. Some splattered against the rock walls, others snarled away in grit-spurting ricochets.

'Get his hoss! We want him alive — for a while!'

Those words surprised Rush. He wheeled the brown, ran it behind a splintered slab of shale. Lead slammed into the shelter and by then he was dismounted and throwing himself down behind a cluster of small rocks.

The rifle lever worked several times and he saw his bullets stitching a line towards brush on top of a rock where he could just make out a man's shirt — looked like the one Candy was wearing. A moment later he had this confirmed: the fat man lurched through the brush, crushing it under his falling weight, his smoking rifle dropping from his hands.

His body rolled down the short, steep slope and ended in a cloud of dust at the bottom. Candy's size had made him a large target: he looked dead, this time. Bonner swung the Winchester in a short arc, searching for Flagg.

Suddenly he heard the whicker of a startled horse, then the clatter of shod hoofs across rock. He had the lever extended and closed it slowly, raising his head in disbelief: Flagg was abandoning the fight!

No guts? Or something else?

It turned out to be something else: a crash of gunfire behind and above him. He twisted over, bringing the rifle with him at the ready and saw the men from the lineshack, Flapjack leading, sliding and fighting their sweating mounts down the slope. It was too treacherous for a quick descent and by the time they reached the level where Bonner was, Flagg had disappeared. One of the riders started over that way but Flapjack called him back.

'Wait up, Cleve! Let him go, or you might end up like that fat man.'

The wrangler turned to Bonner who was standing now. He nodded to the wrangler. 'Nice timing, Flapjack.'

'Luck. Just remembered this snake's nest of gullies in here and seen you makin' for it, not realizin' the danger . . .' As Bonner signalled his thanks by a lifted finger, and lowered the hammer on his rifle, Flapjack's Winchester rose

174

quickly. 'Leather that, Bonner. I'm takin' you back to Marty whether you like it or not.'

★   ★   ★

Horsehoe reined down on a jutting, flat boulder, and shielded his eyes as he saw the small, tight group of riders making their way down a cutting. A dust cloud rose behind them.

'Don't see Bonner's roan among that lot,' he called down to where Dean Halstead was directing the few remaining posse men for a search. 'Too dusty to be sure.'

He snapped his head up at Horseshoe's words. 'He's gotta be there!'

'Not on his roan.'

'Only one set of tracks goin' up an' over that rise, Dean,' reported one of the men Halstead had sent to search for sign. 'Could be Bonner.'

Dean frowned. 'Well, how the hell . . . ? I mean, what the hell happened here? Candy's dead.'

'Not quite, Dean,' called another posse man who had been kneeling beside the fat man. 'Won't last long, though.'

Halstead hurried across and Horseshoe came down from the flat rock, sliding his way across.

Candy had three wounds — one, in the fleshy part of his flabby body under his left arm, was older than the others, which were in his chest and bleeding freely. But the flow was slowing noticeably as his heart laboured.

Candy's pudgy face was a terrible mix of grey and red blotches and his breathing was wet-sounding as he heaved and fought for air. He was obviously afraid of these armed men standing around staring at him.

'Help . . . me.'

'You're past help, fat man,' Halstead said coldly, kicking him hard enough to make the dying man gasp in pain. 'Who got away? Flagg or Bonner?'

Candy stared and there was a hint of malice in his crumbling face as his gaze locked with Dean's: no sign of compassion there. He worked his scummy lips. 'B-Bonner. Dunno where Flagg is — B-Bonner took his mount . . . '

Which would account for the heavy hoofprints left by Flagg's big chestnut. Candy was close to death, but he would have the last laugh, send these lawmen on a wild goose chase. *Flagg would — would be proud of him . . .*

' 'Nother thing.' He was fighting to hold on now but desperately wanted to glimpse their faces when he spoke for the last time. 'The — the money . . . You can have it.'

'What the hell?' Horseshoe said, astounded, and the others looked surprised, too.

'All yours. That ain't what we was after . . . '

It was too much that last. He convulsed and croaked and gasped and Dean Halstead kicked him in frustration.

'Quit that, Dean!' snapped a townsman. 'It — it ain't right!'

The others murmured agreement.

Dean scowled down at the dead man.

'What the *hell* was he talkin' about? Not after the money, for Chris'sakes!'

'Hadn't we better get after Bonner?' suggested Tunstall, the man who had found the hoofprints.

'Yeah, I guess,' Halstead said with an effort. By now, everyone was convinced Bonner had murdered Sheriff Pollard and stolen the money: they had kept him on the run long enough for that. Now it was time for him to die and carry that guilt with him to Hell or wherever he ended up. 'Maybe Bonner knows what it's all about — but be careful! Flagg might be on foot but he'll be stalkin' around here still, could even have linked-up with Bonner. I dunno what the hell's goin' on, but I do know Flagg and Bonner are both goddamn killers!'

Wouldn't hurt any to plant the thought solidly.

'Mount up and let's get this lousy chore done!'

12

M Slash R

'I hope I wasn't mistaken about you, Mr Bonner.'

Marty Rice's face was sober as she bathed the bullet burn across his shoulder blade. He twisted his head slightly and looked up at her.

'You think I murdered Pollard and stole that money?'

'I just said 'I hope I'm wrong' — You've been on the run for a long time. Dean Halstead has no doubt forced the pace but it's obvious he's convinced you're guilty.'

'And you?'

'I'm still not certain. I know little about you. You have to admit, it looks very bad.'

'You should see it from where I'm standing. 'Very bad' doesn't even touch it.'

She frowned, wiped his back and then poured some iodine into the shallow gouge. He sucked in a sharp, hissing breath and smothered a curse. He blew out his lips and looked up at her again.

'Don't look like that — it wasn't intentional! I can't stop iodine from stinging.'

'Guess not. That damn posse kept me on the run but I've had time to figure a few things out — the way it might've happened.'

'Some might say you've had time to think up some lies to cover your tracks.'

Flapjack spoke from where he leaned against the wall of the ranch kitchen near the stove. He was still carrying his rifle. Bonner threw him a hard look, reached for his old shirt but the girl grabbed it before him.

'You can't put that filthy thing over a clean wound! I keep a slop-chest for my crew; I'll find you something better.'

She left the room and Flapjack propped the rifle against the wall, took out tobacco and papers and began to build a cigarette. He tossed the sack to Bonner who caught it with a nod. They were smoking when the girl returned with a red-and-white checked shirt. It had had a couple of repairs but the stitching was neat. She helped Bonner slip into it.

'That concho belt I had with me — is it safe?'

Frowning slightly she looked at Flapjack. He nodded. 'Put it with your gear. You souvenir that from the Mex gunslinger I heard about?'

'I don't rob the dead. He asked me to send some money to his wife in Juarez. Said it's stitched into his belt.'

Marty Rice looked at him sharply.

'You intend to send it to the woman?'

Bonner's face was sober as he met her gaze.

'Told him I would.'

After a moment she said, 'You're on the run, liable to be shot on sight by Halstead's posse, but you — gave your word to a man who must've been trying to kill you only minutes earlier? And you're going to try and keep that promise?'

'You said it. I gave my word.'

The girl glanced at Flapjack who had his lips pursed slightly. He scratched his sweat-flattened hair, shook his head slightly.

'I don't think we made a mistake first time, Marty.'

She smiled slightly and nodded. 'It seems not, but . . . '

'Yeah — but.'

'What's wrong with you two?' Bonner demanded. 'Don't a man's word count for anything in this damn country?'

'Some men's do. Not every man means what he says, Mr Bonner, especially if money's involved.'

'Well, I give my word, I stick by it.' He spoke with a hard edge now, eyes narrowed and challenging, glancing briefly at Flapjack's rifle.

The wrangler moved casually in front of it. 'Maybe you better tell us what you figured out.'

Bonner still looked mildly hostile.

'You must see we have to doubt you, Mr Bonner. We've had nothing to make us think otherwise.'

'Better call me Rush,' he said, in a friendlier tone. 'Yeah, I guess they did a good job of making me look like a murderer and a thief.'

Marty frowned slightly. 'D'you think it was planned? Or was it some spur-of-the-moment thing? And *who?*'

'I like the deputies for it: Halstead and Horseshoe.'

'They're kinda tough,' Flapjack said slowly. 'I've heard they take a little under the table from the saloon and a couple of the unofficial cathouses, but that's normal enough in any cowtown.'

'Ten thousand dollars, stolen, and already blamed on someone else, is more than a few bucks passed under the table,' Bonner said quietly. He tapped his chest. 'I was already a suspect. Kit Pollard was s'posed to be investigating my story of someone stealing my horse and me getting it back with his saddle-bags containing the money from that bank robbery at Miller's Ford.' He shook his head. 'Hell, saying it out loud, it does seem kind of slick.'

'To a lawman and plenty of other people, I suppose so,' Marty told him, 'But it sounds feasible enough to me.'

She looked towards Flapjack who hesitated, and then shrugged his shoulders.

'Guess I was waitin' to see what Kit turned up.'

Bonner smiled thinly. *'Gracias, amigo!* I appreciate your faith. Look, for now just let me tell my story, OK?'

They agreed impatiently and he told about Secombe's treacherous attack on him in his camp, shooting him in the head and stealing his roan. Then the time trying to survive without food or clean water and finding himself in a position to take his roan back and kill Secombe in the process.

'I think Pollard more than half believed me, but he was a careful man and sent his telegraphs, keeping me locked up until he got replies, one way or t'other.'

'Yes, that's how Kit operated. I think I told you at the time he was a hard man, but fair.'

Bonner nodded, smoked silently for a few draws, then said, 'Now this theory: Halstead and Horsehoe put on a little act in front of my cell about handing over the key of the safe and making a point of saying where the key was kept — and that the stolen money was *in* the safe. There were a couple of drunks in one of the other cells who were sober enough to back their story if they needed 'em to prove I knew about those things.'

'Or one of them drunks stole the money and killed the sheriff?' Flapjack couldn't keep the scepticism out of his voice.

Bonner shook his head. 'Halstead and Horseshoe stole the money and one of them killed Pollard. The act outside my cell was so they could say later that was how I knew where to find the key to the safe and had the drunks as witnesses. They should've been on the stage, the way they set it up for my breakout: first they hassled me over a non-existent warrant for my arrest from Cochise County, just to help make me grab the chance to run when it came up. I knew it had to be hogwash.'

'It sounds like they knew exactly what they wanted,' Marty said. 'And really stacked the deck against you.'

Bonner nodded. 'They knew what they were doing, all right. Horseshoe burst in just as Halstead was leaving my cell after supper, yelling something about a wild man tearing up the saloon and Dean had better come right away.'

'That'd be Big Fuzz Carmody, mountain man. I was in town that night, not in the saloon, but I heard and seen some of what happened.'

Bonner held up a hand to Flapjack and continued, 'I reckon the fight was set-up, too, just so Dean could act flustered and in a hurry. He fumbled the door lock and it didn't click into place: all I had to do was push it open.'

Marty frowned. 'Couldn't that have been genuine?'

'Could've; I didn't stop to think one way or the other. I just slipped out and went to the front. Pollard wasn't there, s'posed to be visiting some girl. Dean'd made a point of mentioning that, too. I found my sixgun in a drawer and used a big hunting knife I found to pry open the rifle cabinet. I'd just got my rifle when Pollard came in.'

He saw the tension in them both as he reached this crucial point.

'I pressed back into the shadows. He heard me, came at me, and I knocked him out with the rifle barrel — then got outa there fast as I could.'

There was silence in the kitchen except for the coffee pot beginning to boil. The girl automatically turned and lifted it off with a cloth on the hot handle, set it on a metal trivet, then took down three china mugs. She began to pour the drinks.

'Where was that knife you mentioned?'

Bonner set his gaze on Flapjack's face. 'On the desk where I'd tossed it — it was still there when I left. And, before you ask, the safe was locked or, as far as I know. I never even looked at it: all I wanted to do was grab my guns and go find my horse.'

As she set coffee in front of Bonner and Flapjack pulled out a chair and sat down, Marty said, 'When Dean Halstead went in to open up the jail so they could put Fuzz in, Kit was dead on the floor with the knife in his chest, the safe was open and the money gone.'

'I told you how the office was when I left.'

'And Dean found it very different, Rush.'

Before he could reply, Flapjack said, 'Dean ran on ahead of the bunch carryin' Fuzz — must've been there for quite a few minutes before they arrived. I was on the boardwalk near the saloon when he came out of the law office.'

Bonner nodded. 'I reckon he might've been taking the money out of the safe when Pollard came round. If there was a struggle, Dean could've grabbed the knife off the desk and stabbed Pollard, then hid the money somewhere and ran outside, yelling *murder* with me as the prime suspect.'

They sipped their hot coffee, the girl watching both their faces and then she nodded slowly. 'It's very plausible, don't you think, Flapjack?'

'Yeah. Dean's always been a mean one: he's put a few men in Doc Field's infirmary. Horseshoe's a bad man in a fight, too. Ideal set-up, Bonner. Nailed you nicely.'

'I'm hoping that means at least one of you figures I'm telling the truth.'

'I believe it could have happened that way,' Marty said slowly. 'I'm following my instincts when I say that.'

'Like you did when you brought me into town to the sawbones. However this turns out, I'm mighty grateful for that, Marty. You saved my life.'

She flushed a little and smiled, getting up to fetch some still-warm biscuits. 'I'm glad Flapjack brought you back here but — I'm not throwing you out, you understand, how far behind is the posse?'

'Not far enough. I'd better get under way.' Bonner turned to Flapjack. 'I'll leave the roan with you — you seem to know what you're doing around horses.'

'I hope so! I been callin' myself a wrangler for years. Fetlock's bad sprained, is all. Rest and some special liniment I made and he'll be right in a week.'

'I'd better be long gone by then.'

'Yeah — you better had,' Flapjack agreed.

'Where'll you go?'

'Was on my way to a join a man I rode with in the army — Ben Tyler. He's got a horse ranch across the Divide, near Wolf Creek. There're buffalo there, too, and he figures we might be able to make some money from the hides that can go into the

190

spread. I've done buffalo-runnin' before, down on the Staked Plains, so I'll be adding my experience to the partnership instead of cash — I'm broke.'

'I wouldn't talk about that, Rush. It makes a perfect motive for you stealing that bank money.'

He arched his eyebrows. 'Never thought of that, and speaking of money: you got that Mexican's belt? Like to get that part fixed before I go.' He looked at Marty. 'If I leave the address, will you send it on to Juarez?'

'Of course. I'm glad I listened to my hunch, Rush. A man in your position, who can still find time to honour a promise made to a dying killer, is surely someone to put your faith in.'

Her words gave Bonner a good feeling.

13

The Wrong Man

Flagg was no fool.

If retreat was called for rather than stand-and-fight, he could make such a decision in the snap of his fingers. He wasn't a man who was afraid of death, but he figured he had a lot more of life to experience and enjoy yet — if running meant living a little longer, then so be it.

But he would run only so far.

Like now. He figured he had had Rush Bonner just where he wanted him when that bunch of cowboys showed up. He could see they were tough, were good shots, not like the soft-handed townsmen in Halstead's posse, so he rode out, away from the pursuing bullets.

But, checking his back trail and

seeing a decent-sized cloud of dust, he assumed at first that the cowboys were coming after him. It was only when he lifted to a rise and found a ledge where he could see country he had travelled through without showing himself that he saw clearly who was following him.

The damn posse — and it had shrunk! *Well, well, well . . . how about that?*

So Bonner had ridden off with the cowboys, which meant they would have taken him to that ranch he had glimpsed in the distance. He had seen the partly constructed lineshack, too.

Now maybe *that* was where they had gone, rather than all the way back to the main house. There had been four of them, five counting Bonner, and there were — how many posse? He counted swiftly — looked like six or seven. Halstead, Horseshoe, the rest original posse members from town.

OK! *Let's cut the odds some!* Time was running out — he had to catch up with Bonner soon or the whole shebang would blow up and all the killing and robbing would have been for nothing.

He was down behind a rock at the rim of his ledge even while he was thinking, rifle loaded, a handful of spare cartridges in his sagging shirt pocket. The posse were riding all over the place, spread out — likely that was Halstead's orders — but they would have to bunch to come through the cutting below this rise.

'*Adios,* you sons of bitches!'

The rifle muzzle followed the tight bunch as they squeezed out of the cutting and he was disappointed to see that Dean Halstead and his sidekick had dropped back, let the townsmen ride into whatever might be waiting.

He grinned tightly: that Halstead was a man after his own heart in lots of ways.

But it wouldn't save him! The rifle blasted, raking the riders with four fast, slamming shots, made louder by the walls of the cutting and the underside of the jutting ledge where Flagg lay.

The first man pitched from the saddle, arms and legs flapping as he bounced off a rock — head first. *Forget him!* The second man reined up sharply as his horse faltered and started to go down. He tumbled awkwardly over the mount's head, and hadn't hit the ground before the rider following also found himself in trouble: his horse reared up on to its hind legs, whinnying, wild-eyed, fell sideways, jamming the man's leg against the wall of the cutting. Flagg thought he heard the man's cry of pain but moved the rifle on, glimpsed Dean Halstead and brought the muzzle back, triggering.

But the deputy was a fast thinker, saw what had happened to the men in front of him in a matter of seconds, simply wheeled his mount, knocking another man skewed in his saddle, shouldering his horse past even as Flagg's bullet tore the hat from his head.

Maybe the lead caught some of his hair, for his head and shoulders seemed to jerk and his horse smashed into the rider behind — looked like Horseshoe — and down they went in one hell of a tangle of men and mounts, dust boiling. Through it, he saw the remaining posse men crashing back through the cutting to where no danger lurked.

He got to his knees, searching for Halstead, but the man was smart enough not to try to stand. He was rolling out of the tangle, kicking and punching his way free, flopping in behind a downed horse. The other men were still sorting themselves out and Flagg bared his teeth as he squeezed the trigger again. *Damn! Magazine empty!*

Hunkering down, he fumbled shells out of his shirt pocket, thumbing them home swiftly, dropping only one before he had the tube fully loaded. He jacked one into the breech.

Goddamn! They must have moved fast down there — panic-driven most likely. There was no sign of anyone alive there now. Two men — the first two through the cutting — lay dead and unmoving, and he was sure one other was at least out of it with his smashed leg. Two horses were down for keeps and a third struggled to stand but its hind legs were unable to support its weight.

But the men had gotten themselves under cover somewhere. He half rose, seeking a glimpse of anyone.

The bullets tore a groove in the shale beside his head and he reeled back, face bloody from spurting rock chips. One took him alongside the left eye and he shook his head, heart pounding — thickness of a cigarette paper more and he could have lost that eye!

But Flagg wasn't one to waste time on such things. He tore off his sweaty neckerchief, mopped his face as other lead raked his shelter. *That damn Halstead!* He just knew it had to be him. *Hell, he couldn't even see properly.* Well, that shambles down there wasn't going anywhere right now. By the time they sorted themselves out, argued about who was going back to town and who was staying on — and argue they would . . .

Well, Flagg reckoned to be long gone by that time. He fired a volley to make them keep their heads down, leapt up and around his sheltering rock to where he had left his big chestnut with a rock anchoring the reins.

The mount was tired, but he spurred it away brutally.

* * *

'He's gone, Dean! Can't hear his hoss now, but he'd be shootin' our fool heads off if he was still up there!'

There was a shaky edge to Horse-shoe's voice: they had all come mighty close to being killed in this cutting.

'Well, it sure wasn't Bonner!' gritted Halstead, raking his glance up the slope where Flagg had ambushed them. 'That fat-assed bastard lied with his dyin' breath — sent us after the wrong man!'

'Because you kicked the hell outa

198

him!' snapped one of the surviving townsmen. 'Told you you shouldn't've done it! Just ain't right treatin' a dyin' man that way.'

The man reared back as Dean's rifle muzzle jabbed at him and stopped an inch from his left eye. 'Mebbe I'll treat the next dyin' man I see even worse! You wanna find out, Kerry?'

The townsman was a ghastly colour and shook his head, unable to speak. There was only one other townsman unhurt, and he was treating the third man, who was groaning, his leg crushed and bloody.

'What's the sense in all this?' he snapped, a livery hand named Cassell. 'We're beat, lucky to be alive. Ned here has to have a doctor. I'm takin' him back to town, an' to hell with you, Dean, before you start cussin' me out. I've had enough and you'll have to shoot me to stop me goin'.'

'That's easily arranged!' snapped Dean, swinging his rifle across, but Horseshoe reached out and pushed the barrel groundwards, meeting Halstead's burning stare.

'Cassell's right, Dean. No sense in this kinda thing — we gotta get after Bonner.'

Halstead didn't like being reminded and brought back to the task at hand, but he forced himself to nod slowly. He glared at Cassell and Kerry.

'Go on — git! An' don't expect to pull posse pay for the time you've been with us.'

'We'll see about that! We're entitled to at least three days' pay, an' most of today and we'll get it, too!'

Dean turned his back. 'Horseshoe, get our mounts. We're leavin'.'

'You could lend a hand with buryin' those dead men first!' Cassell snapped. 'Hell, they're *neighbours*, friends — we owe 'em a decent burial.'

'Yeah, guess so,' Dean said quietly. 'You and Kerry can see to it, bein' such upstandin' citizens. Me an' Horseshoe have our own job to do!'

They played it safe and waited a spell

to make sure Flagg wasn't holed-up somewhere, just waiting for them to appear. Then, finally, Dean sent Horseshoe out of the cutting and the man reported back quickly.

'No one here, but his tracks lead back — towards M Slash R!'

'Well, that ain't any real surprise . . . God damn that Candy! We coulda had Bonner by now! C'mon, there's been enough delay. Time we ended this — an' that's just what I aim to do! Once and for all.'

★　★　★

They approached the half-built line-shack warily, Dean Halstead crouched behind a tree, Horseshoe somewhat reluctantly, crouched double, rifle at the ready, as he closed with the rear of the shack. Only part of the wall had been logged-up. Horseshoe could see into the interior where the men who had been working out here had spread their bedrolls and set up their gear.

He stood slowly, rifle angled towards the ground now, thumbed back his hat.

'C'mon on in, Dean. Ain't no one here gonna give us any trouble.'

Halstead was still leery about showing himself, worked his way down and came up on the other side of the partly raised log wall. He peered through a chink between the logs, ready to be sealed with mud, and sucked in a breath as he saw the two bodies sprawled near their bedrolls. Blood had soaked into the ground beneath them, mixed with some wood shavings where one of them had thrashed about a little before dying.

He went around to the end of the wall where Horseshoe waited.

'That damn Flagg. He's a cold-blooded bastard, eh?'

'I'd've done the same,' Dean answered casually. 'No sense in leavin' someone alive if he could put a bullet in your back. Take a look for some tracks.'

'Already have. Don't even have to kneel down to see 'em.' He gestured briefly. 'There, in the loose dirt near the stump they been usin' as a choppin' block. Hoofprints big as a soup bowl. Has to be Flagg's chestnut.'

Halstead nodded: he had seen enough of those prints after finding Candy dying not to need a closer look.

'Headin' for the ranch. The hell's he goin' there for?'

'Bonner.'

'Yeah. Wants that money and figures he's the one run off with it.' He grinned crookedly. 'We set that up pretty damn neat, din' we?'

'Yeah, but Candy said that thing about them not bein' after the money at all.'

Dean scowled and spat. 'And he lied about Bonner takin' Flagg's hoss and sent us on a wild goose chase!'

'Aw — yeah, s'pose he was lyin'. Just didn't seem like it to me.'

'Well it did to me! Now let's get going. Be close to dark when we get to the ranch and that'll suit us fine.'

Horseshoe was slow to move and

Halstead ripped out an oath. 'How many men's Marty runnin' these days, Dean? We could be ridin' into a heap of guns.'

'We're the law, ain't we? Flagg's the one ridin' into trouble. We just doin' our job of pickin' up an escaped prisoner. They ain't gonna give us an argument about that.'

'We-ell, I guess you're right.'

But Horseshoe didn't sound too sure and Halstead snapped, 'C'mon, dummy — They'll hand Bonner over to us or I'll throw 'em all in jail. They know that, from Marty herself on down. They know better'n to fool with me.'

Horseshoe hoped so; he was getting mighty tired of this long chase. What he really wanted, was to collect the money from wherever Dean had hidden it in the law office, divvy it up, and ride on out.

Anything else could be settled later when he was miles away and no longer interested. *Leave it to Dean.*

Halstead had a habit of using everyone.

Well, see how he liked it when there was no one to bully, no one but himself to do the chores.

As if Halstead had read Horseshoe's mind, the big deputy said, casually, but with a sidelong bleak look, 'By the way, I got that money hid good. So you better watch out for me, Horseshoe. I stop a bullet and you're still a poor man.' He broadened his crooked grin. 'No one'll ever find that cash but me.'

Horseshoe didn't say a word out loud, But under his breath he cursed Dean Halstead with every filthy epithet he knew — and made up a few extra as he went along.

Smarter than a snake; but snakes could be killed and some took a long time to die.

14

Alforjas

'You won't get far before sundown, why don't you stay overnight and leave early in the morning?'

Bonner was adjusting the cinchstrap on the horse Marty had given him — this time another roan gelding, bigger than the one he was leaving in Flapjack's care.

'Thanks, Marty, but you've done enough.' He gestured to the saddle and bulging bags and grub-sack. 'If I'm caught here you'll be in a heap of trouble.'

'But you don't know the country, and at night — ' He shook his head stubbornly and she sighed. 'All right. Flapjack'll ride with you to the pass and it should still be light enough for him to point out the best way for you to go after that.'

Rush knew it made sense but he was reluctant to involve these folk any more. Seeing his hesitation, she smiled. 'He's an obliging man and he'll see the sense in it.'

'OK — and thanks again. I dunno how I'll ever be able to square with you.'

'Let me know how your endeavour turns out — when you're a rich horse rancher.'

He smiled back at her and nodded. 'I just might do that.'

★ ★ ★

From back in the trees at the western edge of the spread, Flagg, sitting his chestnut, leaned forward, squinting. He watched Bonner mount and then Flapjack came riding up from the corrals, forking a dun. The girl waved them off and they started across the undulating land, now beginning to show signs of mellow gold light as the sun began its daily slide into the west.

Flagg wiped at his face which was still spotted with blood, a few of the tiny punctures oozing slightly. His eye watered and he scrubbed at it irritably. He still couldn't see all that well. Not too bad close up, but distance was blurred.

Be no good trying to use a rifle with an eye like that; he had always aimed and shot with both eyes open and in something as important as this, he wasn't ready to take the chance. He needed Bonner alive — for a while, anyway — so he had to place his shot just where he wanted it. An inch off and he was likely to kill the man outright and would never get the information he needed.

Feeling the anger churning, he eased back in the saddle, still dabbing the watering eye. There was movement at the ranch house as the girl turned back through the door.

A couple of ranch hands close by were washing-up at the bench alongside the bunkhouse. He scrubbed a hand around his jaw, feeling the rasping stubble.

They likely knew who he was by now: no use trying to put over the US marshal ploy. *Maybe he could pass for a drifter looking for a hand-out . . .*

Maybe.

★　★　★

Marty was stirring a huge pot of rice to which she had added tomatoes and sliced onions, with a couple of liberal dashes of tabasco sauce: her men liked their grub spicy. There were savoury meatballs to go with it. There was a knock on the rear door and she left the stove, slightly annoyed at the interruption.

The man standing at the foot of the short steps wrinkled his nose and squinted up at her. He seemed to have something wrong with his left eye and his face was spotted with blood. Hat in hand, Flagg smiled, but his bad teeth did nothing to make her feel more at ease.

'Ma'am, don't like appearin' on your doorstep just at suppertime, but I've gotten myself lost and — well, that meal sure does smell good.'

Marty was suspicious: he smelled of wild trails but she could also smell gunsmoke on him — his clothes seemed to be saturated with it. The light was bad and the falling sun was behind him. He also kept dipping his head.

She was about to tell him to go wash-up and he could eat in the barn, when suddenly he was forcing her back into the room. She began to struggle as one arm went around her waist. He spun her about and clapped a filthy hand over her mouth. His breath was stale and sour as he spoke close to her ear.

'One sound and I'll bury your face in that boilin' rice.' He laughed briefly, kicking the door closed. 'Don't reckon it'd improve it any — nor you.'

He dragged her, still struggling futilely, through the house to the front door, pushed her on to the porch. He stayed back in the shadows and she heard his Colt hammer ratchet back to full cock. 'Call 'em back.'

She started to turn her head. 'Wh-what?'

'Lady, you're nice-lookin' but I can change that with one drag of the foresight across your face. You heard what I said! Now do it!'

Marty, heart thumping, cleared her throat and cupped her hands around her mouth, calling Flapjack and Bonner. After the third try Bonner hipped in the saddle, then Flapjack as they halted their mounts. She waved her apron with urgent motions.

They hesitated, no doubt puzzled, then turned their horses and came loping back, Flapjack pulling slightly ahead.

'What's wrong, Marty?' he called, as they raced in by the corrals. The other cowhands were gaping from around the bunkhouse door. 'What'd you call us back for?'

Bonner was just skidding his roan to a halt when Flagg stepped out on to the porch, grabbed the girl around the waist and pulled her back against him, the sixgun at her head.

'I don't need you,' Flagg said to Flapjack and fired.

The bullet knocked Flapjack clear off the horse. It whinnied and jumped to one side as the wrangler hit the dirt and flopped on to his side. Bonner's hand had whipped to his gun butt but he froze as Flagg put his Colt to Marty's head again. She looked at Flapjack, horrified, tried to struggle free. 'Let me go to him!'

Flagg shook her hard as the other cowhands came running. But they stopped and lifted their hands when they saw the situation: they had all taken off their guns for supper.

Flagg spoke affably. 'Just stand out there in a group and keep your hands where I can see 'em.'

'No need for this, Flagg,' Bonner said tightly. 'It's me you want. Let's ride away from here and leave these good folk.'

'Shut up, Bonner,' Flagg rasped, eyes squinting, the left one blinking as he tried to clear it. 'I don't want much from you — just a few words.'

'And a few thousand dollars.'

Flagg grunted. 'Well, I wouldn't mind that either, but I'll pass on it if you just gimme the saddle-bags.'

Marty twisted her head to look at him, stunned. Bonner frowned and there was a slight tensing of his lean body.

'The *saddle-bags?*'

'Yeah — the saddle-bags! *Alforjas*, swayback pokes, gunnysacks — you know the ones I mean. Greaser-made leather with a lot of fancy decoration on the flaps. Look mighty nice even when they ain't stuffed with ten thousand bucks.'

Bonner's frown deepened. 'You don't strike me as a man who'd collect such things, Flagg.'

'Shut up, I told you!' Flagg screwed the gun muzzle into Marty's head and she winced and grimaced, finally cried out in pain. 'Come on! I'm tired of this. *Where're the goddamn bags that money was in?*'

Still puzzled, Bonner shrugged. 'Kit Pollard took 'em off me when he threw me in jail.'

'Aaaah! He'd have kept the money in 'em when he put it in the safe! *And you took it, so you got the bags, too!*'

'Wrong, Flagg, I never took that money. *Wait!* Don't hurt Marty. She knows nothing about this. Look, Halstead and Horseshoe framed me for the robbery and the murder of the sheriff — will you just listen long enough while I tell you how they set it up?'

Flagg, despite his misgivings, felt himself being persuaded by Bonner's tone and the way the man looked. 'Can't be much to tell! You busted out, took the cash, killed Pollard and been on the run ever since.'

'More to it than that.' And Bonner swiftly launched into a brief explanation about the deputies' act outside his cell, and how he figured Pollard had been

214

stabbed by Dean when he was caught stealing the money from the safe. Flagg was growing impatient and interrupted several times but Bonner talked over him, finishing with: 'It was a setup to make everyone figure I'd stolen the money and was on the run with it. Halstead likely hid it somewhere in the law office. He aimed to run me down with his posse and kill me and that would've been an end to it. They'd say I must've stashed the money somewhere while on the run.'

'*The hell with the goddamn money!*' Flagg roared, startling them all. 'Judas priest, I'd like that money in my hand, but it ain't the most important thing — them saddle-bags are!'

'They're empty for God's sake, wherever they are!'

Flagg grinned tightly. 'Mebbe they look that way, but I want 'em and you're gonna tell me where the hell they are, or I'll start blowing fingers and toes off this here *muy bueno señorita* until you do!'

Marty was white-faced and struggling, afraid of her captor. Bonner felt helpless: Flagg's gun was only an inch from the girl. Even if he drew faster than he had ever done, she was still in danger of dying — or might be crippled if the bullet hit her spine.

'Flagg — no hogwash. Kit Pollard kept those saddle-bags. That's gospel. You want, I'll ride back to town with you and tear the law office apart till we find 'em, but *I don't have them and don't know where they are!*'

'Then that makes her mighty unlucky!'

Flagg chuckled and, frantic now, Marty got one hand between her back and Flagg's body. She felt his crotch, hesitated, then grabbed and squeezed and twisted as hard as she could.

The onlookers were as startled as Flagg — but not in as much agony. The killer screamed, doubled up and reeled drunkenly. His legs gave way, his face contorted, flecks of foam and vomit on his lips.

Rush Bonner drew and fired twice.

His lead lifted the killer off his feet, hurled him into the rails. They splintered and gave way, his body falling into the yard.

Marty's legs gave way, too, and she sat down, heart hammering as if it was trying to smash its way out of her chest. Bonner leapt off his mount, smoking gun covering Flagg, calling to the stunned cowhands.

'Tend to Flapjack. I just saw him move.'

As they ran to obey, he kicked Flagg's gun under the porch, leapt up the steps and knelt beside the girl. She was fighting for breath and he held her shoulders firmly.

'That's it — deep breaths. Slow and easy, Marty, slow and deeeep . . . '

He felt her settling down and while she gathered herself, he reloaded his Colt.

'Is — is Flagg — ?'

'Dead and ready for burial. That was a mighty fine move you made.'

She flushed, pushed some hair off her face. 'I was terrified . . . I just reacted.'

'And in the best way. Look, Marty, he'd've killed us all and not fast. He was crazy to get his hands on those damn saddle-bags.'

'But why?'

'There must be something hidden in them somewhere. Whatever it is, it must be worth a lot more than the ten thousand dollars from the bank . . . though I'm not sure he wouldn't've tried to get his hands on that money anyway.'

He helped her to her feet and she leaned back against an awning post, looking down to where the cowhands had Flapjack's shirt open. Blood glistened on his pale skin in the dying light. 'Is he alive?'

'Yes, ma'am. Bullet got him in the left side, still in there, I guess. There's a mighty big knot on his head. Reckon he lit on that and it's what knocked him out.'

'Get him into the parlour, Lonnie. You help carry him, Les, and Burt can get some hot water and rags from the kitchen.' She glanced at Bonner. 'I'll need to work on Flapjack right away. If you want to continue for the hills, or if you'd rather stay overnight — '

'Thinking mebbe I will stay. Halstead'll show up sooner or later and you'll need someone to back you — '

'She won't need you, Bonner!'

Bonner whirled at the sound of Horseshoe's voice as he rounded a corner of the house, cocked rifle in hand. The deputy lifted the gun quickly, fired, and Bonner spun as lead burned his upper arm. He dropped to one knee and his Colt blasted Horseshoe off his feet. The man tried to spin towards the porch, rifle smoking, and Bonner shot him again. He slammed back, wide eyes staring at the slowly darkening sky.

Bonner stood, a thin line of blood creeping across the back of his left hand and starting to drip from his fingers. The cowboys who had been carrying Flapjack through the doorway had crouched low and he spilled from their grip. They were startled to hear him curse.

'Flapjack!' Marty said, her eyes lighting up, her lips smiling as she knelt beside him. 'Don't try to move — '

'Tell these idjuts that!' he gritted, indicating the cowpokes who had dropped him. Then he nodded. 'I — I'm hurtin', Marty, but I'll be OK . . . '

'I wouldn't bet on it!'

Dean Halstead came up the porch steps, ignoring Horseshoe's body, cocked Colt covering Bonner.

'I could shoot you where you stand and be within my rights.'

'There're a lot of witnesses, Dean!' Marty pointed out tightly.

'Sure — witnesses that this wanted murderer shot down my deputy in the performance of his duty! I'm outnumbered by folk I believe to've helped him dodge my posse. No court would blame me for puttin' a bullet into him just to be on the safe side.'

Bonner was tense, his gun down at his side. When Dean jerked his Colt he let it fall with a thud near the white-faced Flapjack who seemed to have passed out again. Rush lifted his hands to waist level: he didn't want any more lead flying around here with Marty and her men bunched so tightly together.

Now it seemed to be Dean Halstead's move.

'Heard a little of what you told Flagg — about me and Horseshoe framin' you. Quick thinkin', I guess, but a load of crap.' He flicked his gaze briefly to Marty and smiled thinly. ' 'Scuse me, Marty. It ain't true. Bonner's the killer and the thief. Mebbe he didn't mean to kill Kit but he done it and stole that money from the safe; that makes for a 'Dead or Alive' warrant.'

Bonner said nothing and Marty started to argue with Halstead but gave up when she saw he was only toying with them. He knew he could shoot Bonner in cold blood and get away with it, without having to admit to any wrong-doing himself where the money was concerned and certainly not Kit Pollard's murder.

'You — you won't get away with it, Dean!' Marty spoke because she felt she had to, knowing it was futile.

Halstead gave her his attention — and suddenly Flapjack scooped up Bonner's Colt from beside him, holding it in both shaking hands, fumbling to cock the hammer. Halstead shot him and Bonner rammed into the deputy, sending Halstead flying off the porch to spill into the yard.

Bonner rolled across the porch, snatched the Colt from beside Flapjack's still body. He spun as the deputy reared up, swinging his sixgun. Rush triggered, an unaimed shot but diversionary, twisted on to his belly, elbows tight against the porch floor, and fired twice more, the hammer notching back for the third shot — but it wasn't needed.

Dean Halstead jerked, shaking, his legs buckled and he fell to his knees. Bonner fired again anyway, and the bullet spun Halstead, knocking him on his face in the dirt.

* ★ ★

They made a night run into town, carrying both Flapjack and Horseshoe in a buckboard to the infirmary.

Their arrival disturbed the doctor at his supper and he was not a happy man when he saw the blood-spattered men — and the trail-weary, stubbled Rush Bonner lurking in the background.

'I assume this is some of your doing.'

'Some.' Bonner gestured to Horsehoe. 'It's all Dean Halstead or Horsehoe's lead in Flapjack. Give him priority, Doc. He's worth more than ten Horsehoes.'

'I'll decide who has priority, Mr Bonner,' the sawbones said curtly, examining the men, lifting the blood-soaked rags Marty had used as bandages. He sighed. 'I can't say much more than that they're both alive. I'm not sure I can save either one.'

'Save 'em both and everyone'll be happy.'

The doctor frowned as he looked sharply at Bonner. Then he nodded slowly. 'Of course — Horseshoe can clear you if your story is true.'

'You still tend to Flapjack first, Doc.

'You don't intimidate me, Bonner!'

'Well, I guess I'm not trying to. But I owe Flapjack a helluva lot; I owe Horseshoe nothing.'

'I understand, but I will bring in my good wife and we'll tend to both men.'

'I'd like to help, Doctor,' Marty said.

'I think my wife's nursing skills will be needed here, thank you all the same, Marty. Why don't you and Bonner search Kit Pollard's office? You might find the money *and* the saddle-bags.'

Bonner liked that idea well enough, but as Marty nodded, reluctant to leave Flapjack, the doctor said, 'Wait — it might be as well to have a reliable witness with you. No, no, I'm not suggesting either of you would try to keep the money but — well, people talk, and Bonner's still in a position that could see him at the wrong end of a rope. Take a lawyer with you.'

'Could be you're right, Doc, but

where'll you find a lawyer this time of night?'

'There's only one successful one in town, Sean Fisher. He's a go-getter and won't pass-up the chance at an extra dollar — a *few* extra dollars, for the inconvenience, actually. My wife can prepare the patients. I'll get dressed and see if I can fetch Sean.'

★　★　★

Fisher was neatly and fully dressed when the doctor brought him back. His frock coat wasn't even wrinkled and his shirt was silk, with a blackstring tie, the crease in his striped trousers sharp enough to cut a finger, and his boots polished.

His hair was naturally curly so that probably hadn't required any attention. He held his hat in front of him, didn't offer a hand to Bonner when introduced, but bowed very slightly towards Marty.

'Yes, we've done business in the past,

have we not, Miss Rice?'

'We have — and satisfactorily, Mr Fisher.'

Another slight bow. Bonner had detected a trace of brogue from the man's ancestors in his speech, but his brisk manner spoiled the effect of what should have been easy-going tones.

'I have a key to the law office.' Everyone looked blank and Fisher smiled gently, taking a brass key from a pocket of his vest. 'Sheriff Pollard thought it prudent to leave a spare key with me — for emergencies.'

He turned and hurried out and Marty only shrugged at Bonner's uncertain glance and they followed.

Fisher hovered about, not touching anything, leaving the search to the girl and Bonner.

'Careful!' he snapped, as Marty went to step around the bloodstains still on the floor where Pollard had fallen and stumbled against the desk. An unlit lamp started to fall but she caught it deftly. 'We must not damage anything.'

Bonner straightened from looking under a desk that was raised a few inches from the floor. 'We might have to tear up some floorboards to find the money.'

'Carefully, Mr Bonner. If it is necessary, we will do it carefully.'

'Would Dean Halstead have had time for that?' Marty asked and they both agreed he likely had not.

'He could've stuffed it in the saddle-bags and put them up in the roof.' Bonner gestured to the ceiling and trap door leading to the roof space. He started to pull a chair beneath the trap and the lawyer, frowning, said, 'What saddle-bags are you talking about?'

Setting the chair, Bonner said shortly, 'The Mexican ones they found the money in.'

'You can save yourself a climb, Mr Bonner. I saw Kit Pollard carrying such *alforjas* over his arm. I believe he was on his way to see his *paramour*.' He said this last with distaste. 'A half-breed

Lakota dancer . . . '

'Winnie Lake-Flower,' Marty said tightly, glaring at Fisher. 'She's a very good dancer, Counsellor, and a nice person, although a little hostile towards white men.'

'We-ell — eye-of-the-beholder and so on, Miss Rice, but I did see the sheriff with those bags.'

'Then we gotta go see this dancin' woman.' Bonner stepped down from the chair and turned towards the door.

Marty stopped him. 'Rush, you killed her brother, remember.' Lawyer Fisher stiffened. 'Oh, it was in self-defence, Counsellor! Billy-Bob Cougar was trying to kill Rush. I'd better go and see Winnie. She might be more willing to speak to me.'

'Ye-es,' Fisher said slowly, 'but she lives in a rather rough section of town. Perhaps Bonner ought to accompany you, Miss Rice — stay in the background, of course, but I think it would be wise.'

'I'm not afraid to walk through the

red light district.'

'Nonetheless . . . '

'He's right, Marty. I'll follow and wait outside.'

'Make sure she can't see you, then,' Marty agreed somewhat reluctantly and they went out.

The lawyer seated himself in the chair and took a tortoiseshell and silver cigar case from his inside coat pocket. He smiled. 'You're paying me by the hour . . . '

★　★　★

Bonner was mighty tense by the time Marty came out of the now darkened cabin where the 'breed woman lived.

She wasn't carrying the saddle-bags!

He stepped out of the shadow of the building where he had waited just down the street and Marty took his arm, urging him back to Main. 'Where're the bags?'

'She has them. There was a double gusset in one. This was hidden between the leather.' She held up an oblong of paper, folded several times. 'She apparently collects bric-à-brac: the cabin's full of odd little china ornaments and Spanish fans of various designs, purses and so on — '

Bonner wasn't interested in that. 'What's the paper? Must be dynamite if it's worth what Flagg reckoned.'

'I haven't looked at it yet. Thought it best to leave it for Sean Fisher.'

Lawyer Fisher opened it right away, cigar clamped between his teeth, the aromatic smoke filling the small room.

'My God!' he exclaimed huskily as he read.

'*He* already knows what's in there — we don't,' growled Bonner impatiently. He reached for the paper but Fisher pulled it out of reach.

'I'm not sure I should allow you to see this . . . it might be best all round if I simply destroy it.'

'Mister, I've been on the run for what feels like half a damn year. I've been shot; beat-up; I've starved and gone

230

almighty thirsty; near-crippled the best horse this side of the Rio and — gimme that damn paper! If I have to take it off you, you won't walk outa here as spry as you walked in, I give you my word!'

'Rush!' Marty said urgently as she saw Fisher go pale, stepping back hurriedly. 'I believe we've earned the right to know what's in it, Counsellor.'

Fisher, wide eyes on Bonner, nodded and proffered the paper: it rustled because his hand was shaking.

'It — it's obviously been torn from a Court Records book — at least fifteen years old — a youthful indiscretion that could so easily destroy him. What it was doing in the bank vault, I have no idea, but obviously whoever Flagg worked for knew about it. I'd go so far as to say the money was stolen as a cover-up, 'pickings' for the thieves, but that this paper was the main object of the theft.'

Bonner frowned. Marty, studying the paper, gasped. 'Good Lord! Payne Harbison! Of all people . . . '

'Who's Payne Harbison?' snapped

Bonner and they both stared at him.

'Where have you been, man?' Fisher said sharply, regaining his composure. 'It's only weeks since the hardest-fought, dirtiest election campaign in the history of Montana Territory! Surely you know that Payne Harbison is the Governor-elect! A fine, fine man who will guide this territory to full statehood within a couple of years . . . '

Bonner shrugged. 'I ain't interested in politics.'

'That's obvious! Don't you realize that if Payne Harbison is not inducted that the way will be open for his opponents to put up their own man — Wade Melchoir? He has foreign connections, wealthy Europeans just waiting in the wings to exploit this country to the full and fill their own coffers while they're doing it? It — it's unthinkable!'

'Dammit, Fisher! I said I'm not interested in politics — and I still don't know what's in that goddamn paper that's got your tail in a knot!'

Marty, wanting to head off trouble, thrust the paper towards Bonner. He almost snatched it, and read slowly. Fisher showed signs of impatience as the minutes passed but Marty signed to him to wait. Eventually, Bonner glanced up, handed the paper back to Fisher.

'Yeah — burn the damn thing. I can savvy enough to figure that if Harbison's enemies got their hands on this he'd be finished. But, hell almighty! He was only barely into his twenties when he killed that man!'

'Yes, but it was the husband of the woman involved. She had played on his youthful infatuation.'

'Did he serve that prison sentence?'

Marty answered. 'I recall my mother speaking of it. They wouldn't allow the woman to testify in court — they could do that in those days. She must have had genuine affection for young Harbison, though. She committed suicide, left a sworn affidavit to say her husband had planned Harbison's murder for cuckolding him, but it had gone wrong and her husband had become the victim while Harbison was only trying to protect himself.'

'It's the scandal, you see,' Fisher said, seeing Bonner's frown. 'Not whether he served time in prison or not — married woman, young man aspiring to a political career. Dynamite without the fuse.'

Bonner nodded. 'Yeah, I see. Got a match . . . ?'

* * *

They found the money up in the roof of the law office and Fisher offered to handle negotiations with the Miller's Ford Bank for a reward to be paid to Bonner.

'I shall take my usual ten percent commission, of course.'

'Would never have thought otherwise, Counsellor.'

Fisher had also bullied, threatened and finally terrified Horseshoe into agreeing to admit his part in the whole deal, the lawyer pointing out with cold logic, 'You were not present when the sheriff was murdered; though a prosecutor of my own experience could no doubt imply, if not prove, your complicity and then the hangman's knot would be a foregone conclusion. Or a defence counsel could get you a prison sentence. Not pleasant to contemplate, but you'd still be alive . . . '

That sounded good enough to Horseshoe.

Rush turned to Marty. 'Looks like I'll be able to put some cash into Ben's horse ranch after all.'

She smiled. 'I'm glad. It'll keep you in the one place while you build up the spread into a paying proposition.'

Looking thoughtful he nodded. 'Yeah — guess so.'

But didn't hear her say under her breath, 'And I'll know just where to find you.'

Other titles in the
Linford Western Library:

HELL'S COURTYARD

Cobra Sunman

Indian Territory, popularly called Hell's Courtyard, was where bad men fled to escape the law. Buck Rogan, a deputy marshal hunting the killer Jed Calder, found the trail leading into Hell's Courtyard and went after his quarry, finding every man's hand against him. Rogan was also searching for the hideout of Jake Yaris, an outlaw running most of the lawlessness directed at Kansas and Arkansas. Single-minded and capable, Rogan would fight the bad men to the last desperate shot.

SARATOGA

Jim Lawless

Pinkerton operative Temple Bywater arrives in Saratoga, Wyoming facing a mystery: who murdered Senator Andrew Stone? Was it his successor, Nathan Wedge? Or were lawyers Forrest and Millard Jackson, and Marshal Tom Gaines involved? Bywater, along with his sidekick Clarence Sugg, and Texas Jack Logan, faces gunmen whose allegiances are unknown. The showdown comes in Saratoga. Will he come out on top in a bloody gun fight against an adversary who is not only tough, but also completely unforeseen?

PEACE AT ANY PRICE

Chap O'Keefe

Jim Hunter and Matt Harrison's Double H ranch thrived . . . till their crew marched away to war's glory, and outlaws destroyed everything and murdered oldster Walt Burridge. When the war ended, the two Hs started over. However, for Jim, war had wrought changes beyond endurance. So Jim rode out and into the arms of his wartime love, the gun-running adventuress Lena-Marie Baptiste. Now, trapped by his vow to avenge Old Walt, he must choose between enmity and love, life and death.

SIX DAYS TO SUNDOWN

Owen G. Irons

When his horse is shot dead, Casey Storm is forced to brave a high plains blizzard. Stumbling upon a wagon train of Montana settlers, he helps them to fight their way toward the new settlement of Sundown. But gunmen hired by a land-hungry madman follow. Now the wagon train's progress seems thwarted by their pursuers and the approaching winter. With only six bloody days to reach Sundown, will Casey's determination win through to let them claim their land?

MISTAKEN IN CLAYMORE RIDGE

Bill Williams

Ben Oakes had always been involved in trouble — he'd killed men before — but now he was determined to live a new life and never to carry a weapon. But when he's wrongfully imprisoned for the murder of Todd Hakin, he's desperate to clear his name and escape the hangman's noose. Then Ben is finally released, and his search for Todd's killer leads him to Claymore Ridge, where he faces threats to his life from more than one quarter . . .

TWO FOR TEXAS

Ethan Flagg

The Texas cattle town of Buckeye has been taken over by outlaw boss Wade Garvey. When his men start turning up with their throats cut, he brings in the hired gunfighter known as Nevado to find the killer. However, all is not what it seems in Buckeye, and amidst simmering passions, an unlikely liaison forms between Nevado and the mysterious knife-wielder . . . Then, as the bullets begin to fly on Nob Hill, it all culminates in an explosive climax.